Usborne
Children's
World
Cookbook

Angela Wilkes and Sarah Khan

Edited by Fiona Watt and Kirsteen Rogers
Illustrated by Nadine Wickenden
Food photography by Howard Allman

Designed by Michael Hill, Karen Tomlins
and Joanne Kirkby

Contents

(V) suitable for vegetarians   * contains nuts

Internet links

For downloadable versions of these recipes and links to websites where you can find out more about cookery around the world, go to the **Usborne Quicklinks Website** and enter the keywords **"world cookbook."**

Hints and tips

Before you try any of the recipes in this book, read it all the way through to make sure you have all the ingredients and equipment you will need. You should be able to buy all the ingredients in a big supermarket, but you could also try specialty or ethnic stores or markets.

Cooking words

Here are some of the cooking words and techniques that are used in the book.

- **For how many?**
  The recipes in this book are enough for four people unless the recipe says otherwise.

- **Measuring**
  Measure the dry ingredients in measuring cups, and liquids in liquid measuring cups.

- **Cups or ounces?**
  Some of the ingredients are given in both cups and ounces. You can use either measurement.

- **A spoonful**
  In this book, a "spoonful" means a level spoonful.

- **A pinch**
  A "pinch" means the amount you can pinch between your thumb and your forefinger.

- **Using an oven**
  When you put things into an oven to cook, put them onto the middle shelf, unless the recipe says something different. Move the shelves to the right position before you switch on the oven.

- **Convection ovens**
  If you have a convection oven, you will need to turn it to a lower temperature than the one shown in this book. Follow the instructions in the oven's manual.

SIMMERING

Cooking a liquid over low heat so that it bubbles gently, but doesn't boil.

SIFTING

Shake flour or sugar through a sieve to get rid of lumps and make it light and airy.

CHOPPING AN ONION

1 Halve the onion. Lay each half, cut-side down onto a chopping board and make cuts across it.

2 Turn the onion. Cut across the first cuts at right angles, so that you chop it into small pieces.

BEATING

Stir as hard as you can with a wooden spoon until the mixture is pale and creamy.

WHISKING

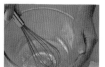

Move the whisk around and around, very quickly. Hold the bowl with one hand as you do it.

Put ingredients onto a clean chopping board before you cut them with a knife.

SEPARATING AN EGG

1 Gently crack the egg on the edge of a bowl. Pull the shell apart, keeping the egg in one half.

2 Tip the yolk from one half to the other, so the white slips into the bowl. Put the yolk into another bowl.

KNEADING

1 Use the heels of both hands or your knuckles to push a ball of dough away from you.

2 Fold the dough in half and turn it around. Push it away from you, as you did in step 1.

3 Keep folding, turning and pushing the dough until it feels smooth and stretchy.

RUBBING IN

Mix butter and flour by rubbing them with your fingertips until they look like breadcrumbs.

FOLDING IN

Use a metal spoon to slice into the mixture and turn it over and over until it is evenly mixed together.

GREASING

Rub a baking pan or oven-proof dish with butter, oil or non-stick cooking spray to keep food from sticking.

MAKING BROTH

1 Boil some water in a kettle. Cut up or crumble a bouillon cube. Put it into a liquid measuring cup.

2 Pour in the amount of boiling water you need. Stir it well until the bouillon cube dissolves completely.

Be safe

- Whenever you find it difficult to do something, ask someone to help you.

- Be very careful when you are slicing things with a sharp knife. Always put the ingredients onto a chopping board.

- Always put on oven gloves before picking up anything hot or when putting things into or taking them out of the oven.

- Don't leave the kitchen while electric or gas rings are on.

- Wash your hands thoroughly after handling raw meat, and cut meat and vegetables on separate chopping boards.

- When you have finished cooking, put everything away and clean up any mess. Leave the kitchen tidy.

The United States of America

The United States of America is a huge country made up of 50 states. Over the last 300 years, people have come to live there from all over the world, bringing their traditional recipes with them. Many of these dishes have gradually changed over time, and their modern forms are now seen as being typically American.

New York delis

New York is famous for its delicatessens. These are small shops that sell sandwiches, salads, cold meats and other snacks. Many delis specialize in particular types of food, such as Italian or Jewish food.

New York is known as "the city that never sleeps" because many of its restaurants, takeouts and delis are open until the early hours of the morning.

These twisted knots of baked dough are a popular snack, called pretzels. They're based on an old German recipe brought to the U.S. by immigrants in the 1700s.

New York cheesecake

This delicious creamy cheesecake is based on a traditional Jewish recipe. It contains eggs and cream, which makes it different from other types of cheesecake. You will need an 8 inch round springform pan.

Ingredients

- ⅓ cup butter
- ⅔ cup graham crackers, crushed into crumbs
- 3 eggs
- 12oz. cream cheese
- ⅓ cup sugar
- ⅔ cup whipping cream
- juice of 1 lemon
- 1 tablespoon cornstarch

✱ Oven temperature: 300°F

If you want to decorate the top of your cheesecake, sprinkle it with grated lemon peel or some powdered sugar.

1 Melt the butter in a pan on low heat. Turn off the heat. Stir the cracker crumbs into the butter.

2 Turn on the oven. Grease the cake pan. Dump the crumbs into it and press them down firmly with a spoon.

3 Bake the cracker crust for 20 minutes. Meanwhile, separate the eggs into two different bowls.

4 Beat together the cheese and egg yolks. Mix in the sugar, cream, lemon juice and cornstarch.

5 In a separate bowl, whisk the egg whites until they form firm peaks. Use an electric mixer if needed.

6 Use a metal spoon to fold the egg whites gently into the cheese mixture until they're mixed in.

7 Pour the mixture onto the crust and smooth it level. Put it in the oven to bake for 50-55 minutes.

8 Turn off the oven. Leave the cheesecake inside to cool. This will keep the top of the cheesecake from cracking.

Chocolate brownies

Chocolate brownies are American cakes. They are crisp and crunchy on the top and slightly gooey in the middle. Traditionally they are made with walnuts or pecan nuts, but leave them out if you can't eat nuts, or replace them with the same quantity of chocolate chips if you prefer.

Ingredients

- 6oz. (²/₃ cup) walnuts or pecans
- 4oz. semi-sweet baking chocolate
- ²/₃ cup butter
- 1 cup sugar
- 1 teaspoon vanilla
- 3 eggs
- ½ cup flour
- 1 level teaspoon baking powder

- A cake pan-
  9x12in and 1in. deep

★ Oven temperature: 350°F

Walnuts

Pecans

1 Grease the cake pan. Put it onto baking parchment. Draw around the pan, cut out the shape and put it in the bottom.

2 Turn on the oven. Put the nuts into a plastic bag. Roll a rolling pin over them to break them up.

3 Break the chocolate into a heatproof bowl. Stand the bowl over a pan of simmering water.

4 Cut the butter into pieces and stir them into the bowl of chocolate until everything melts.

5 Pour the melted chocolate and butter into a mixing bowl. Stir in the sugar and vanilla.

6 Whisk the eggs in a bowl. Beat them into the chocolate mixture bit by bit, using a wooden spoon.

7 Sift the flour and baking powder into the bowl and add the nut pieces. Mix together well.

8 Pour the mixture into the cake pan. Smooth the top with a knife and bake it for around 40 minutes.

9 Let the mixture cool a little. Cut it into squares, then leave the brownies on a wire rack to cool.

Brownies are good eaten the day you make them, but they will keep for a day or so in an airtight container.

Pumpkin pie

Pumpkin pie is a traditional dessert in America. Mashed or puréed pumpkin is mixed with eggs and cream and baked in a pastry pie. It's eaten on Thanksgiving Day, a national holiday.

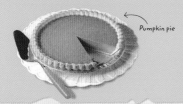

Pumpkin pie

Pumpkins grow on long, sprawling vines. A single vine can grow as long as 10m (30ft), sending out around 10 to 12 shoots from which the pumpkins grow.

Canada

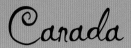

Canada is the second largest country in the world. Vast areas of land are used for farming, and huge lakes and a long coastline provide fish and other seafood. Canadian food is influenced by the United States and also by Europe, because of the many British and French people who moved there.

These are maple leaves. They are the national emblem of Canada.

Maple syrup

Maple syrup is a national specialty of Canada. It's made from the sap of maple trees, which is collected from the trunks, then boiled to make a sweet, runny syrup.

This type of maple tree is called a sugar maple. It grows well in cool, moist climates, such as those found in southeastern Canada.

To collect sap from maple trees, tubes are drilled into the trunks and the sap slowly drips out into buckets. The roof you can see keeps the rain out.

Canadian pancakes

Canadian pancakes are small and puffy with crisp edges. In Canada, people often eat them for breakfast with maple syrup.

Ingredients

For 8-10 pancakes

- 1 cup flour
- 1½ teaspoons baking powder
- 1 egg
- 8 tablespoons vegetable oil
- 1 cup milk
- maple syrup

1 Sift the flour and baking powder into a bowl. Mix, then make a well in the middle with a spoon.

2 Carefully break the egg into another bowl. Whisk it with two tablespoons of the oil and all of the milk.

3 Beat the egg mixture into the flour, a little at a time, until everything is mixed and makes a smooth batter.

4 Pour two tablespoons of the oil into a frying pan and heat it gently until a faint haze rises from the pan.

5 Carefully spoon two tablespoons of batter into the pan to make one pancake. Add batter to make two more.

6 Cook the pancakes for about a minute on one side. When they begin to bubble, turn them over with a spatula.

7 Cook the pancakes for another minute, until they puff up. Pour more oil into the pan to cook more pancakes.

The pancakes are best served piping hot with maple syrup poured on top.

Latin America

Latin America is the name given to Mexico and all the countries in Central and South America. It has vast areas of land used for farming beef cattle and growing crops, such as corn. Latin American food is hot and spicy. The main ingredients are tomatoes, chili peppers, corn and beans.

These freshly made wraps have been stuffed with spicy meat and beans from the pans, ready for the lunchtime rush at a Mexican food market.

Tacos

Tacos are corn or wheat wraps filled with a spicy meat mixture and a variety of toppings. Tacos can be made with soft, floury wraps, called tortillas, or hard corn shells, called tostadas. You can find soft tortillas and hard taco shells in supermarkets.

1 Turn on the oven. Chop the onion and crush the garlic. Cut the lettuce into strips. Slice the tomatoes.

2 Heat the vegetable oil in a large pan. Cook the onion and garlic over low heat until they are soft.

The lettuce, tomato and sour cream add a cooling contrast to the spicy meat underneath.

3 Turn up the heat. Add the meat to the pan. Cook it, stirring it all the time, until it is brown all over.

4 Add the tomato purée, cinnamon, chili pepper, salt and pepper. Cook it over low heat for about ten minutes.

5 Stand the tacos on a baking sheet. Put them in the oven for three minutes so that they warm up.

6 Spoon some of the meat into each shell or tortilla and add lettuce, tomato and a tablespoon of sour cream on top.

Serve the tacos with bowls of guacamole, salsa and refried beans, so that people can help themselves to the toppings. The recipes for these are on the next page.

Ingredients

- 1 medium onion, peeled
- 1 clove of garlic, peeled
- a small head of lettuce
- 4 tomatoes
- 2 tablespoons vegetable oil
- 1lb. ground beef
- 1 tablespoon tomato purée
- 1 teaspoon cinnamon
- a pinch of mild chili pepper
- a pinch of salt and of black pepper
- 8 taco shells
- sour cream

- a baking sheet

✳ Oven temperature: 350°F

Guacamole

Tomato salsa

Refried beans

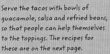

Guacamole

Serve this creamy avocado dip with tacos. You will need really ripe avocados, which are soft when you press them. It's best to eat guacamole on the day that you make it.

Ingredients

- 2 tomatoes
- 2 ripe avocados
- a few drops of chili sauce
- juice of half a lemon
- a pinch of salt and of black pepper

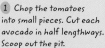

1 Chop the tomatoes into small pieces. Cut each avocado in half lengthways. Scoop out the pit.

2 Scoop the avocado flesh into a bowl. Then, mash it into a smooth, thick paste with a fork.

3 Mix all the other ingredients into the avocado. Beat the mixture until it's smooth.

Tomato salsa

In Latin America, spicy sauces called salsas are served with many dishes, including tacos. Some are made with hot chilies. For this recipe, let the salsa stand for about an hour after you have made it. This brings out its full flavor.

Habañero chilies are the hottest chilies you can get.

Jalapeño chilies are fairly hot. They are traditionally used in salsas.

Ingredients

- 4 ripe tomatoes
- ½ small red onion
- a handful of fresh cilantro
- a few drops of chili sauce
- juice of half a lime
- salt and black pepper

1 Put the tomatoes into boiling water for two minutes, then into cold water for two minutes.

2 Skin the tomatoes, then chop them finely. Cut the ends off the onion. Peel it, then chop it finely.

3 Chop the cilantro. Mix all the ingredients together in a bowl, then let the salsa stand for an hour.

Refried beans

Latin American cooks use beans in lots of different ways. This recipe uses kidney beans to make a dish to serve with tacos.

Ingredients

- 1 medium onion
- 1 clove of garlic
- 1 tablespoon vegetable oil
- 14oz. can red kidney beans
- a pinch of salt and of black pepper

1 Peel the onion and chop it finely. Peel the clove of garlic, then crush it.

2 Heat the oil in a frying pan until a haze rises. Cook the onion and garlic over low heat until soft.

3 Drain and rinse the beans in a sieve, then add them to the pan. Mash them into the onions and garlic with a fork.

4 Fry the bean mixture until it is hot all the way through. Stir it to keep it from sticking. Add the salt and pepper.

5 Spoon the mixture into a bowl. You can sprinkle grated cheese over the top, or use it as a filling for tacos (see pages 12-13).

You can dip corn chips into refried beans, guacamole or salsa.

Bean feast

Black beans and black-eyed peas are popular all over Latin America, and are used in soups, stews and sauces. Many Mexican dishes include red kidney beans, particularly hot, spicy stews. You can use most types of beans to make refried beans. Make sure you soak dried beans overnight before you use them.

Red kidney beans   Black-eyed peas   Black beans

15

Fruit

There are many kinds of fruit, growing all over the world, and you can find a wide selection of them in stores and supermarkets. Some might look strange, but they're all worth trying. You never know what delicious new tastes you might discover.

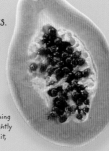

Pawpaw (papaya) — a sweet, juicy fruit which is ripe when it's slightly soft. Halve it and remove the seeds before eating the flesh. Don't eat the skin.

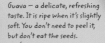

Guava — a delicate, refreshing taste. It is ripe when it's slightly soft. You don't need to peel it, but don't eat the seeds.

Passion fruit — ripe when its skin is dark and wrinkled. Cut it in half and eat the juicy flesh and seeds.

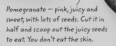

Pomegranate — pink, juicy and sweet, with lots of seeds. Cut it in half and scoop out the juicy seeds to eat. You don't eat the skin.

Sharon fruit (persimmon) — looks a little like a tomato. It's ripe when soft, and tastes very sweet. You can eat it whole or scoop out the flesh to eat.

Star fruit (carambola) — has a delicate, but sharp flavor. It's ripe when its edges are slightly brown.

Pineapple — ripe when it smells sweet, but not too strongly. Cut off the skin and cut out the core, then slice the flesh.

Kumquat — tastes a little bit sour. Eat them whole without peeling them.

Physalis — a slightly bitter fruit. It's ripe when soft. Pull back the papery leaves and eat the whole berry.

Tamarillo — a red fruit with a bitter taste. It can be eaten raw or cooked. It's ripe when slightly soft.

Mangosteen — ripe when its skin is dark purple. Slice through the thick skin, pull the halves apart and scoop out the sweet flesh.

Mango — a very sweet fruit. It's ripe when slightly soft. Page 19 shows you how to cut one open.

Lychee (litchi) — sweet, juicy, and ripe when soft. Peel off the skin and eat the white flesh.

Kiwi — can be eaten by peeling and slicing it, or cutting the top off and eating the inside.

Horned melon (kiwano) — tastes a little like cucumber. Halve it and eat the seeds inside.

The Caribbean

The Caribbean, also known as the West Indies, is made up of hundreds of tropical islands famous for their blue seas, white sands and coral reefs. Over the centuries, different peoples have settled there, each bringing their own traditions. Caribbean dishes are a spicy and exciting mixture of African, Asian and European cooking, using fresh seafood, chicken, rice, beans and fruit.

Mangoes grow on trees, ripening during the dry summer months. They have to be picked before the rainy season comes, or they'll rot on the branches.

Mango fool

A fool is made from puréed fruit. It's important to use ripe mangoes in this recipe. They should have a strong scent and should "give" a little when you press them lightly.

Ingredients

- 2 ripe mangoes
- 1 lime
- 1 teaspoon honey
- ⅔ cup whipping cream
- 5oz. plain yogurt
- 1 tablespoon coconut milk

Tall coconut palm trees, like these, grow on all the islands in the Caribbean.

1 On a chopping board, slice the mangoes lengthways, on either side of the big pit in the middle.

2 Make cuts along and across the flesh, as shown, then slice the chunks of mango away from the skin.

3 Put the mango flesh in a bowl and mash it with a fork until it becomes smooth.

4 Cut the lime in half and squeeze out the juice. Stir the juice and honey into the mango purée. Mix well.

 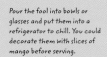

5 In another bowl, whisk the cream until it starts to thicken. It shouldn't form peaks.

6 Stir the yogurt and the coconut milk into the mango. Then, gently fold in the cream so that everything is mixed.

Pour the fool into bowls or glasses and put them into a refrigerator to chill. You could decorate them with slices of mango before serving.

Banana bread

People eat and cook bananas in many different ways in the Caribbean. They are eaten fresh, baked, boiled or fried. In this recipe, they are made into moist banana bread. This is a dessert bread, more like a cake in some ways than bread. It is best eaten buttered, while still slightly warm.

Ingredients

- ½ cup softened butter
- ⅓ cup sugar
- ⅓ cup brown sugar
- 1 cup whole-wheat flour
- 1½ teaspoons baking powder
- a pinch of ground nutmeg
- 3oz. raisins
- ⅓ cup chopped walnuts

- 1 egg
- 2 tablespoons milk
- 2 large bananas
- 1 teaspoon vanilla

- a 1 pint loaf tin

* Oven temperature: 350°F

This sweet loaf isn't just a snack. It's also served alongside soups and stews.

1 Turn on the oven. Lightly grease the loaf tin with butter. Line its base with baking parchment.

2 Cut the butter into cubes and put them into a bowl. Add both types of sugar and beat well with a wooden spoon.

3 Continue beating the butter and sugar until the mixture is pale, soft and creamy.

4 Sift the flour, baking powder and nutmeg into another bowl. Add the raisins and walnuts.

5 Beat the egg and milk together in a cup. Beat them into the butter mixture, a little at a time.

6 Fold the flour mixture gently into the butter mixture, with a metal spoon, until everything is mixed well.

7 Peel the bananas. Put them in a bowl and mash them with a fork. Add the vanilla and stir it in.

8 Stir the mashed banana into the cake mixture, then pour it into the loaf tin. Use a knife to smooth the top.

9 Bake the banana bread for one hour, or until a skewer comes out clean when you push it into the loaf.

10 Let the bread cool in the tin for five minutes, then carefully turn it out onto a wire rack and leave it to finish cooling.

Harvesting bananas

Bananas grow in tropical countries. They are picked while they're not quite ripe, so that they ripen by the time they are sold.

There are hundreds of different types of bananas, that can be red, green or yellow. Some kinds even taste like apples. Plantains are large, green bananas that are cooked and eaten in savory dishes (see page 27).

Bananas grow on long stalks which hang down from trees. A single stalk can hold between 100 and 300 bananas, and weighs 40-45kg (85-100lbs).

Africa

Africa is a huge continent, with over 50 countries. African food is based on the ingredients that are grown or farmed locally. Lamb, goat, rice, wheat, root vegetables, chili peppers, and a variety of spices are common in most parts of Africa.

Many North African dishes are served with couscous, which is made from wheat. Cooks stuff it into fresh vegetables, such as peppers, or use it as a side dish.

Tagine

Tagines are meat and vegetable stews that are served mainly in Morocco, North Africa. There are lots of different recipes for tagines and, although they are all savory, many include fruit, such as apricots or prunes, in the ingredients.

You can serve the tagine with couscous, and vegetables such as carrots and zucchini. Sprinkle the dish with fresh cilantro leaves before serving.

Dried apricots

Ingredients

- 1 large onion
- 1 red pepper
- 4 skinless, boneless chicken breasts
- 2 tablespoons canola oil
- 1 clove of garlic
- 1 chicken bouillon cube
- 1 cup water
- 14oz. can chopped tomatoes
- a pinch of saffron
- ½ teaspoon ground cinnamon
- ¼ teaspoon ground ginger
- a pinch of ground black pepper
- 1 orange
- 12 dried apricots
- 14oz. – 1 large can – chickpeas

1 Peel the onion and chop it finely. Cut the top off the pepper and chop the rest into strips. Then, cut the chicken into strips.

2 Put a tablespoon of the oil into a large saucepan. Heat it for 20 seconds over medium heat and add the chicken to the pan.

3 Keep stirring the chicken for five minutes, until it has changed color all over. Then, take it out of the pan.

4 Put a tablespoon of oil into the pan. Add the onion and cook it over low heat until soft, stirring regularly.

5 Peel and crush the garlic. Add the garlic and red pepper to the pan. Cook it for five minutes, over medium heat.

6 Make the bouillon. Stir the tomatoes, saffron, cinnamon, ginger and black pepper into it. Put the chicken back into the pan.

7 Pour the bouillon over the chicken. Grate the zest from the orange using the small holes of a grater.

8 Cut the orange in half and squeeze out the juice. Add the orange juice and zest to the pan.

9 Halve the apricots. Add them to the pan. Pour the chickpeas into a sieve or colander over the sink and wash them.

10 Add the chickpeas to the pan, put a lid on it and simmer for 20 minutes, stirring occasionally.

Peanut bread

Peanuts are known as groundnuts in Africa and are one of the main crops grown. They grow best in light, sandy soil, in places that are warm and dry. Peanuts are used in lots of different African dishes, including cakes, soups, stews and sauces. This recipe uses chopped peanuts to make a type of bread.

Ingredients

- 2oz. unsalted, shelled peanuts
- 1 tablespoon groundnut or canola oil
- 1½ cups flour
- a pinch of salt
- 3 teaspoons baking powder
- 1 egg

- 1 cup milk
- ⅓ cup sugar
- 2 tablespoons honey

- 2 cake pans, 7x11in. and 1½in. deep

✱ Oven temperature: 350°F

1 Put the peanuts on a cake pan. Roast them in the oven for eight minutes. Wipe oil over the other pan to grease it.

2 When the peanuts have cooled, put them into a plastic bag and roll a rolling pin over them to crush them.

3 Sift the flour, salt and baking powder into a large mixing bowl. Break the egg into a cup and beat it with a fork.

4 Add the egg and peanuts to the flour mixture. Then, mix the milk, sugar and honey together in another bowl.

5 Stir the milk mixture into the flour mixture, then spoon it into the baking tray. Smooth the top.

6 Bake the bread for 30-35 minutes, until the top is golden brown. Let it cool a little, then cut it into rectangles.

7 Using a spatula, carefully lift the slices onto a wire rack. Leave them to cool completely.

If you can only get peanuts in their shells, twist the shell to break them open. There are usually two peanuts in each shell.

African grains

In Africa, people eat a lot of grains and root vegetables. In many places, they grind maize or corn and then cook it to make a thick kind of porridge called "mealie meal." They also grind dried cassava roots into a type of flour to make bread and dumplings.

Groundnut paste

In West Africa, people cook with a smooth and buttery paste made from groundnuts. They use it to make soups and add it to chicken or vegetables.

This family in Zimbabwe are turning their corn into flour. The woman is kneeling to sift it, while her mother and son are pounding it with wooden poles.

The peanut bread will keep for several days if you store it in an airtight container.

Vegetables

Vegetables come from different parts of plants; some are roots, others are shoots, pods or leaves. Big supermarkets usually have a wide selection of vegetables from around the world. Other good places to look are whole food stores, or ethnic markets.

Cassava — a root vegetable, eaten mainly in tropical areas. It's peeled, then the white flesh is boiled, fried, or dried and made into flour.

Avocado — actually a fruit, as it contains a large seed, but eaten in savory dishes. It's ripe if it is slightly soft. Cut it in half, pull it apart, remove the seed and peel off the skin.

Kohlrabi — tastes like a sweet turnip. Peel it, then cut it into chunks and steam or boil it.

Squashes — often stuffed and baked, or boiled and then mashed. There are many types of squashes, and each one has its own delicate flavor.

Acorn squash

Fennel — tastes a little like aniseed. Cut off any damaged outer leaves and slice it thinly. Use it raw in salads, or cooked.

Chicory — crisp white leaves with a slightly bitter taste. Cut off a slice at the root end, then rinse the leaves. It can be used raw in salads, or cooked.

Pak-choi (bok choy) — a Chinese cabbage with dark green leaves and juicy stems. The stalks and leaves can be chopped and stir-fried.

Butternut squash

Spaghetti squash

Sweet potato — a root vegetable. Usually baked, mashed or roasted. It is confusingly known as a yam in the United States (see below).

Okra (ladies' fingers) — eaten as a vegetable or cooked in stews. Trim off the stalks and cook gently in butter or oil.

Plantain — a type of banana, but bigger and savory. It is eaten as a vegetable and used in savory dishes, especially in the Caribbean and Africa.

Mangetout (snow peas) — tender pea pods which are eaten whole. Trim off their stalk and tail. Eat them raw in salads, or steam them so they are still slightly crunchy.

Asparagus — can be green or white and has a delicate flavor. It is steamed or boiled and served hot with a butter sauce as a starter, or cold with salad dressing.

Yam — popular in Africa, the Caribbean, and South and Central America. It is peeled, then boiled or baked and mashed with spices, or cooked like potatoes.

France

France prides itself on its delicious food. Each
region has its own specialties. For example,
Quiche Lorraine, a pastry dish filled with eggs,
cream and bacon, comes from the Lorraine
region in Eastern France. Normandy, in
Northern France, is one of the main apple-
growing areas of the country. It's also known
for dairy products, such as butter and cheese.

Many varieties of apples, such as red and green
Arianes, dark red Juliets and golden green
Chanteclers, were first grown in France.

French apple tart

In France, you can buy fruit tarts, pastries
and cakes at pastry shops called pâtisseries.
Each region has its own special tarts – this
one comes from Normandy.

In spring, French apple orchards
look like a sea of white blossom. The
flowers develop into fruits in summer.

Ingredients

- 1¼ cup flour
- ⅓ cup chilled butter
- 6 tablespoons sugar
- 1 egg yolk, beaten
- 2-4 tablespoons cold water
- 1lb. cooking apples
- 3 eating apples

- 2 tablespoons apricot
  preserves
- 2 tablespoons hot water

- an 8 inch flan dish

✱ Oven temperature: 400°F

1 Sift the flour into a large mixing bowl. Cut the butter into small pieces and add them to the flour.

2 Rub the butter into the flour until the mixture looks like breadcrumbs. Add two tablespoons of the sugar.

3 Mix in the egg yolk and enough water to make a ball of dough. Put it in a refrigerator for 30 minutes.

4 Turn on the oven. Peel the cooking apples, cut them into quarters and cut out the cores. Slice the quarters.

5 Put the apples, cold water and sugar in a pan. Stir them over low heat until the apples are soft.

6 Sprinkle flour onto a board and rolling pin. Roll the pastry into a big circle about ¼in. thick.

7 Line a tart pan with the pastry. Prick it with a fork. Trim the edges with a knife. Bake it for ten minutes.

8 Spoon the cooked apple into the pastry shell. Slice the eating apples and arrange them in circles on top.

9 Mix the preserves with the hot water and brush it over the sliced apples to glaze them. Bake the tart for 30 minutes.

The tart can be eaten hot or cold. You could serve each slice with a spoonful of whipped cream.

Salade niçoise

This is a tasty tuna salad which was first made in Nice in the South of France. Its name means "salad from Nice," and it includes local ingredients, such as tomatoes, anchovies and juicy black olives. Eat the salad with fresh French bread.

Ingredients

- 1lb. new potatoes
- 2 eggs
- 4oz. French beans
- 6 tomatoes
- 1 can anchovies
- 1 crisp head of lettuce
- 14oz. can of tuna

- 3 tablespoons of olive oil
- 3 teaspoons wine vinegar
- ½ teaspoon French mustard
- a pinch of salt and of black pepper
- 2oz. pitted black olives

You can fill a roll or piece of crusty bread with the salade niçoise ingredients. Eat it straight away so the bread doesn't go soggy.

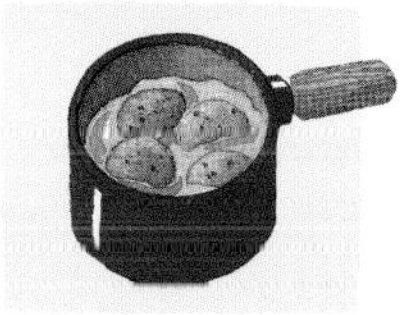

1 Scrub the potatoes. Cook them in boiling water for 15 minutes until tender. Drain, then let them cool.

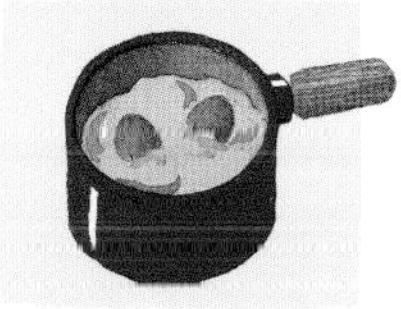

2 Boil the eggs for ten minutes. Put them in a bowl of cold water to cool. Peel off the shells.

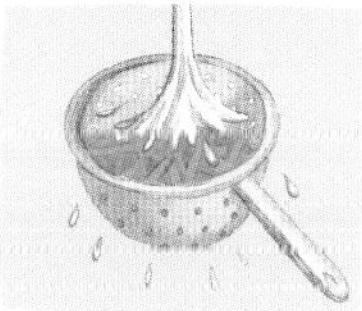

3 Trim the ends off the beans. Boil them for five minutes, then rinse them with cold water.

4 Cut the tomatoes into quarters. Slice the potatoes. Drain the anchovies and cut them in half lengthwise.

5 Wash the lettuce leaves in cold water. Pat them dry and arrange them in the bottom of a large salad bowl.

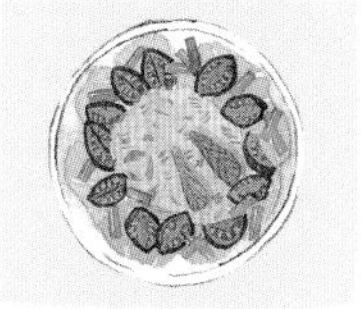

6 Put the potatoes on top of the lettuce. Drain the tuna and put it on top. Add the beans, tomatoes and anchovies.

7 For the dressing, put the olive oil, vinegar, mustard, salt and pepper into a jar. Screw on the lid and shake it really well.

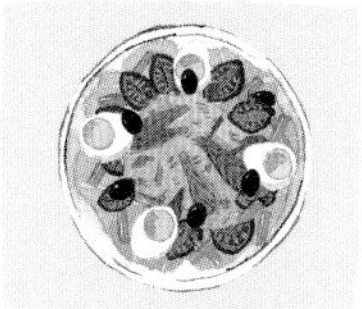

8 Drizzle the dressing over the salad. Slice the eggs, or cut them into quarters. Put them into the bowl, along with the olives.

Markets

If you visit a French market, you may spot the kinds of ingredients that are included in many of the local recipes. For example, in the Alps, you'll see mouthwatering French cheeses, and in Brittany, in the northwest of France, you'll find lots of different kinds of seafood.

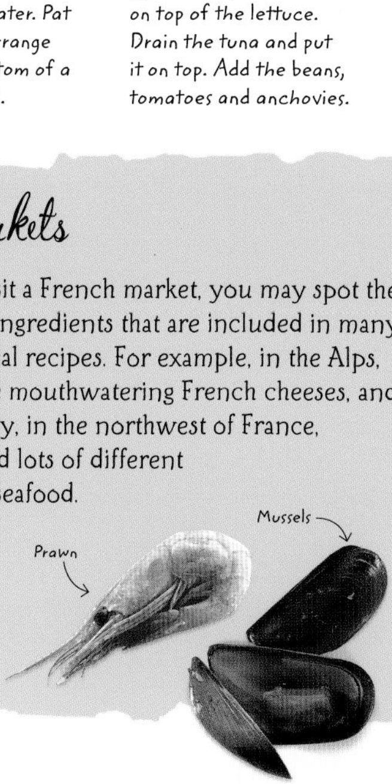
Mussels
Prawn

This fruit and vegetable stall is part of a street market in Brittany. Markets like these are held at least once a week in most French towns.

Spain

Spain is dotted with mountains and hills in the north, and sun-baked plains and beaches in the south. Spanish food has been influenced by the Arabs who lived there for over a thousand years, and by Spanish explorers who brought back ingredients from their journeys.

Paella

Paella is Spain's most famous dish. Rice is slowly cooked with chicken, seafood and saffron to create a filling meal. To make paella, you will need a large frying pan with a lid.

Ingredients

- 1 medium onion
- 1 red pepper
- 6 tomatoes
- 1 clove of garlic
- 2 skinned chicken breasts
- 2 tablespoons olive oil
- 1 chicken bouillon cube
- 1 cup risotto or long grain rice
- 3 cups boiling water (2 cups only if using long grain rice)
- a pinch of salt and of black pepper
- 1 teaspoon saffron threads
- 4oz. peeled prawns (or shrimp)
- 2oz. frozen peas
- 6 fresh mussels

Prawns

Mussels

Tomatoes

The paella is ready when the rice is tender and the mussels have opened. Never try to eat mussels that haven't opened – just throw them away.

1 Chop the onion finely. Core and slice the red pepper. Chop the tomatoes. Peel and crush the garlic.

2 Cut the chicken into thin strips. Heat the oil in a frying pan. Fry the chicken until it is golden brown.

3 Remove the chicken. Fry the red pepper, onion and garlic over low heat until soft. Add the tomatoes.

4 Make the broth in a measuring cup. Pour it into the pan. Stir in the chicken, rice, saffron, salt and pepper.

5 Put the lid on the pan. Cook the paella over low heat for about 15 minutes, stirring occasionally.

6 Stir in the prawns (or shrimp) and peas. Arrange the mussels on top. Cook the paella for five more minutes.

Peppers →

Saffron

Saffron looks like scraps of orange-colored thread, but it's the most expensive spice in the world. It's made from the stigmas of purple saffron crocuses which grow in Spain. The country is one of the world's largest producers of saffron.

Stigma

Saffron crocus →

Crocus stigmas are picked by hand and then dried, which turns them from plump tubes to the fine dry threads that you can see in this bowl.

33

Fish and seafood

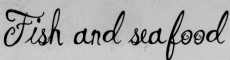

Fish and seafood are the main ingredient in recipes from coastal areas all over the world. If you visit a fish market you'll see the types of fish that are caught locally. Fish can be prepared in lots of different ways — baked, grilled, steamed or fried, to name just a few. In some countries they are dried, or preserved in salt.

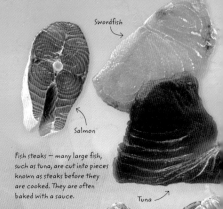

Swordfish

Salmon

Fish steaks — many large fish, such as tuna, are cut into pieces known as steaks before they are cooked. They are often baked with a sauce.

Tuna

Langoustine (Dublin Bay prawn) — break off the tail and pull it apart to get at the delicious white flesh inside.

Shrimp — shellfish with a delicate flavor and firm flesh. They turn orange when they are cooked.

Lemon sole — a flat fish with a light flavor and texture. It's cooked whole or cut into boneless "fillets."

Mussels — tasty shellfish which are sold fresh in their shells. When cooked, the shells open to reveal the flesh inside.

Crab — lots of different types. They are boiled, then the shell is cracked open to remove the flesh.

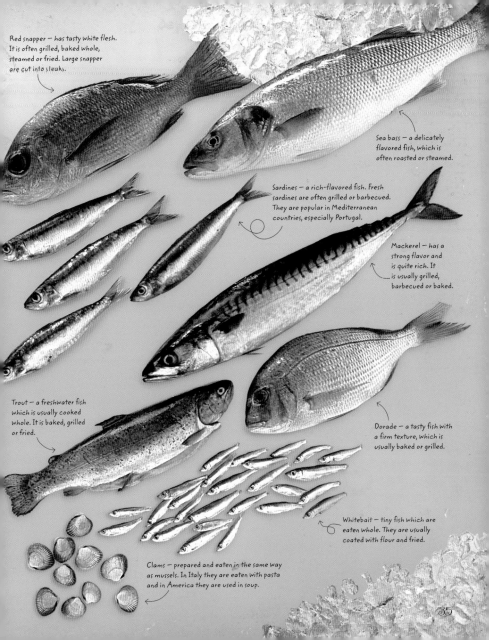

Red snapper – has tasty white flesh. It is often grilled, baked whole, steamed or fried. Large snapper are cut into steaks.

Sea bass – a delicately flavored fish, which is often roasted or steamed.

Sardines – a rich-flavored fish. Fresh sardines are often grilled or barbecued. They are popular in Mediterranean countries, especially Portugal.

Mackerel – has a strong flavor and is quite rich. It is usually grilled, barbecued or baked.

Trout – a freshwater fish which is usually cooked whole. It is baked, grilled or fried.

Dorade – a tasty fish with a firm texture, which is usually baked or grilled.

Whitebait – tiny fish which are eaten whole. They are usually coated with flour and fried.

Clams – prepared and eaten in the same way as mussels. In Italy they are eaten with pasta and in America they are used in soup.

Italy

Italy is famous for its pasta, pizzas and ice cream. There's an enormous variety of other dishes too, each based on the fresh food produced locally, and each region has its own specialties.

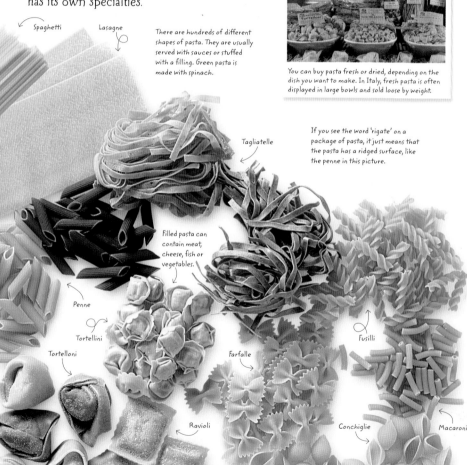

There are hundreds of different shapes of pasta. They are usually served with sauces or stuffed with a filling. Green pasta is made with spinach.

You can buy pasta fresh or dried, depending on the dish you want to make. In Italy, fresh pasta is often displayed in large bowls and sold loose by weight.

If you see the word 'rigate' on a package of pasta, it just means that the pasta has a ridged surface, like the penne in this picture.

Filled pasta can contain meat, cheese, fish or vegetables.

Spaghetti

Lasagne

Tagliatelle

Penne

Tortellini

Tortelloni

Farfalle

Fusilli

Ravioli

Conchiglie

Macaroni

Spaghetti bolognese

This well-known spaghetti dish is served with a meat-based pasta sauce that was first made in the northern Italian city of Bologna. Don't overcook the spaghetti. It should be "al dente" – soft on the outside but still firm inside.

Ingredients

- 1 medium onion, peeled
- 1 medium carrot, peeled
- 1 stick of celery, peeled
- 7 strips of bacon (optional)
- 1 clove of garlic
- 2 tablespoons olive oil
- 1lb. ground beef

- 14oz. can chopped tomatoes
- 2 tablespoons tomato purée
- a pinch of dried oregano or mixed herbs
- salt and black pepper to taste
- 12oz. dried spaghetti
- 1 cup parmesan cheese

Sprinkle some finely grated Parmesan cheese onto the sauce before you serve it.

1 Chop the onion, carrot and celery finely. Cut the bacon into narrow strips. Peel and crush the garlic.

2 Heat the oil in a large saucepan. Cook the onion, carrot, celery and garlic over low heat until soft.

3 Add the ground beef and bacon. Cook until the meat has browned, stirring all the time.

4 Stir in the canned tomatoes, tomato purée and oregano. Taste the sauce and season it with salt and pepper.

5 Put the lid on the pan and let the sauce simmer for 30 minutes. Stir it from time to time.

6 Meanwhile, heat some water in a large saucepan for the spaghetti. Add a pinch of salt.

7 When the water boils, gently push the spaghetti down into the pan until it is covered with water.

8 Boil the spaghetti for 9-12 minutes. Drain it in a colander over a sink. Serve right away with the sauce.

Pizza

Pizzas are now known all over the world, but they originally came from southern Italy. This recipe is for a basic pizza, topped with tomato sauce and cheese. Allow at least 1 hour to make this pizza, as you have to leave time for the dough to rise. The recipe makes a 12in. pizza, which is enough for two.

Ingredients

For the crust:
- ⅓ cup all-purpose flour
- a pinch of salt
- 1½ teaspoon sugar
- ½ teaspoon dry or powdered yeast
- 1 teaspoon olive oil
- 2fl. oz. hot water

- a baking sheet

For the tomato sauce:
- 1 clove of garlic, peeled
- ½ tablespoon olive oil
- 7oz. can of chopped tomatoes
- a pinch of dried oregano

- 2oz. grated cheese, such as cheddar or mozzarella

✱ Oven temperature: 400°F

You can try adding different toppings to your pizza. Here are some suggestions:

Red pepper, sliced black olives and anchovies

1 Sift the flour, salt and yeast into a bowl. Mix them together, then add the olive oil and water.

Pepperoni and basil leaves

Mozzarella cheese and cherry tomatoes

2 Mix everything to make a ball of dough, using a wooden spoon first, then squeezing it with your hands.

3 Sprinkle flour onto a work surface. Put the dough onto it and knead it for five minutes, until it is smooth and stretchy.

4 Grease a bowl and put the dough into it. Cover the bowl with a clean cloth and put it in a warm place for an hour.

5 Turn on the oven. Check the dough. When you see that it has doubled in size, knead it again for a few minutes more.

6 Put the dough on a greased baking tray. Press it into a circle about 12in. across and 1/2in. thick.

7 Crush the garlic. Fry it in a pan with the olive oil, then add the chopped tomatoes. Cook for 10 minutes. Leave it to cool.

8 Spread the tomato sauce over the pizza crust. Sprinkle it with oregano and grated cheese. Add any topping you like.

9 Bake the pizza on the top shelf of the oven for 12-15 minutes, until the edges are golden and the cheese is bubbling.

Italian delicatessens

You can find Italian delicatessens in most large cities around the world. They're usually stocked with a huge range of traditional Italian foods, such as pasta, cheese and meat, as well as cans of olives and vegetables preserved in olive oil.

Olives

Many Italian delicatessens have impressive displays of sausages and hams on their shelves and counters, and even hanging from their ceilings.

Mediterranean ingredients

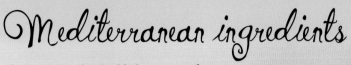

The countries by the Mediterranean Sea
– from Spain right across to Greece and the
Middle East – have a warm, sunny climate.
All kinds of vegetables and herbs
grow well there.

Tomatoes – these form one
of the main ingredients of
Mediterranean cooking. They
come in many sizes and are
used to make salads and sauces.

Capers – these berries are
used to add a sharp flavor
to many dishes, such as fish,
pizzas and sauces.

Sweet peppers – have a mild
flavor and can be eaten
raw or cooked. They
can be red, green,
yellow or orange.

Zucchinis – these are baby marrows. They
are usually sliced then steamed or fried.

Eggplant –
sometimes known
as "aubergine." It is
usually sliced and fried
or grilled until soft.

Artichokes
— usually boiled,
the flesh from
the leaves and
the soft heart
are eaten.

Herbs

Herbs, such as rosemary, thyme, oregano, bay and basil, grow in Mediterranean countries. They are an important ingredient in meat and fish recipes.

Rosemary

Thyme

Bay leaves
— used fresh or
dried, bay leaves
add flavor to
sauces.

Oregano

Rosemary, thyme and
oregano — these herbs are
used fresh or dried. They
are chopped finely and
added to many dishes.

Basil — goes very well
with tomatoes. French
and Italian cooks rip the
leaves into pieces and use
them in sauces, soups and
sprinkled over salads.

Onions — there are several
kinds of onions. They are
usually cooked and used to
add flavor to food. Red
onions are sweeter and
milder than other onions.

Lemons — both the fruit and juice are used
widely in Mediterranean cooking. They are
squeezed, sliced and sometimes used halved.

Olive oil

Pressed from the pulp of olives, olive oil is used for cooking and to make salad dressings. You can taste its rich flavor in many Mediterranean dishes.

Olives — these are the fruit of the olive
tree. Black olives taste similar to green
ones, but are riper and more juicy.

England

Traditional English dishes include fish and chips, roast beef and Yorkshire pudding, and a variety of cakes and "puddings," or desserts. There are dairy farms all over the country and each region makes its own kind of cheese.

Cream teas

Cream tea – a traditional specialty from the south of England – is a light afternoon meal made up of scones, clotted cream, preserves and a pot of tea. The preserves served in a cream tea are usually strawberry or raspberry.

There are many kinds of preserves available in stores all over England. Some people also make their own preserves at home using fresh fruit.

Berries, such as raspberries and strawberries, sometimes grow in the wild, but they are widely cultivated on fruit farms. At some farms, people can pay to pick berries for themselves.

Scones

There's a variety of ways to make scones. This recipe is for the type of sweet scone served as part of a cream tea. It makes 8-10 scones.

Ingredients

- 1 cup self-rising flour
- 1 teaspoon baking powder
- 1½ tablespoons sugar
- 3 tablespoons unsalted butter
- ½ cup milk

- a baking sheet

✱ Oven temperature: 425°F

Cut the scones in half and spread them with preserves and whipped cream.

1 Turn on the oven. Sift the flour, baking powder and salt into a mixing bowl. Stir in the sugar. Then, cut the butter into cubes.

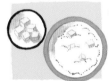

2 Rub the butter quickly into the flour mixture with your fingers until the mixture looks like fine breadcrumbs.

3 Add most of the milk a little at a time, stirring it into the flour mixture with a knife with each addition. Then, flour your hands.

4 Gently knead the mixture until it makes a smooth dough. Add more milk if the mixture seems dry. Leave the dough to rest for 10 minutes.

5 Sprinkle flour on a work surface and rolling pin. Roll out the dough until it is about ³/₄in. thick.

6 Use a 2in. cookie cutter to cut circles out of the mixture. Squeeze the trimmings. Roll them again.

7 Cut out more dough circles. Put them on a greased baking sheet. Brush their tops with a little milk.

8 Bake the scones near the top of the oven for 10-12 minutes, until golden brown. Let them cool on a wire rack.

Ireland

Ireland is a beautiful country with green hills, lakes and a spectacular coastline. Dairy farming and potato-growing have been part of Irish life for hundreds of years. Many traditional dishes have potatoes as an ingredient. There are potato cakes, potato pancakes and even potato bread.

Irish stew

This casserole can be made with lamb or beef, topped with slices of potato. It is cooked slowly at a low temperature, so the meat becomes very tender and the juices simmer to make a tasty gravy.

Ingredients

- 1½lbs. stewing lamb or beef
- 1½lbs. medium potatoes
- 2 large onions
- dried thyme or mixed herbs
- salt and black pepper
- broth made from 1 beef bouillon cube and 2 cups of boiling water
- 2 tablespoons butter

- a casserole dish with a lid

✴ Oven temperature: 325°F

Here you can see potato plants growing in a field. The potatoes themselves grow below ground.

1 Carefully trim any fat off the meat. Cut the meat into cubes about 1in. thick. Turn on the oven.

2 Peel the potatoes and cut them into thin slices. Peel the onions and chop them into small pieces.

3 Put a layer of meat in a casserole dish. Sprinkle on a little thyme, salt and pepper. Add a layer of onions.

4 Add a layer of potato and more layers of meat, onions and potatoes. Sprinkle each layer with the seasoning.

5 Pour the bouillon into the dish. Melt the butter in a pan. Brush it over the top layer of potatoes.

6 Put the lid on the dish and put it in the oven for two hours. Remove the lid for the last 30 minutes.

When the stew is cooked, the potatoes turn brown and are crisp at the edges.

45

Holland

Holland is also known as The Netherlands, which means the low lands. Most of the country is flat, especially the polders, which are areas of land reclaimed from the sea. Dutch food is famous for the cheeses it uses, especially Edam and Gouda.

In Holland, cauliflowers are one of the few types of locally grown vegetables sold in the winter months, because they can grow in cold temperatures.

Cauliflower in cheese sauce

You can make this recipe with any strong-tasting cheese, such as Cheddar cheese, but to give it a really Dutch flavor, use Gouda or Edam.

Ingredients

- 4oz. (1 cup grated) cheese
- 1 large cauliflower, with leaves removed
- 2 tablespoons butter
- 2 tablespoons all-purpose flour
- 1 cup milk
- a pinch of salt and of black pepper
- a pinch of grated nutmeg

This cheese shop is in the Dutch town of Alkmaar. The town has a long tradition of cheese selling and has hosted a cheese market every week since 1593.

1 Grate the cheese. Cut out the core of the cauliflower. Cut the rest into four pieces.

2 Melt the butter in a pan over low heat. Add the flour and stir it to make a smooth paste.

3 Cook the mixture for a minute. Take the pan off the heat. Stir in the milk, a little at a time.

4 Put the pan back on low heat and cook the sauce for five to ten minutes, stirring constantly.

5 Heat a large pan of salted water. Boil the cauliflower in it for five to six minutes, until tender.

6 Use a colander to drain the cauliflower in a sink. Then put the cauliflower into an ovenproof dish.

7 Stir most of the grated cheese into the sauce to melt. Add a pinch of salt, pepper and grated nutmeg.

8 When the cheese has melted, pour the sauce over the cauliflower. Sprinkle the rest of the cheese on top.

9 Turn on the broiler. Broil the dish for a few minutes, until the top bubbles and turns brown.

Serve the cauliflower cheese while it's hot. Be careful as you lift the dish out of the broiler.

Germany

Germany's landscape ranges from the flat North Sea coast to valleys, forests and mountains in the south. German food varies from one end of the country to the other too, but it is mostly warming and homely. Specialties include different kinds of sausages, "spätzle" (noodles), thick soups, dumplings and rye bread.

Lebkuchen

Lebkuchen are spicy German cookies that are baked around Christmas time and decorated with icing. Traditionally they are heart-shaped, but you can get other shapes too. The cookies are ofen hung on Christmas trees as decorations, although they then can't be eaten afterward. This recipe will make about 15 small cookies. Double all the quantities if you want to make more.

Ingredients

- 1 egg
- ¼ cup honey
- ¼ cup butter or margarine
- ¼ cup soft brown sugar
- 1 cup all-purpose flour
- 1 teaspoon baking powder
- 2 tablespoons cocoa powder
- 2 teaspoons ground ginger
- 1 teaspoon allspice

- ⅓ cup powdered sugar
- 1 tablespoon lemon juice

- a baking sheet
- food coloring (optional)
- icing bag or wax paper folded into a cone shape

✱ Oven temperature: 400°F

1 Grease a baking sheet with butter. Separate the egg, putting the yolk into a bowl. Turn on the oven.

2 Put the honey, butter and sugar into a pan over low heat. Stir until the butter has melted.

3 Sift the flour, baking powder, cocoa powder, ginger and allspice into a bowl. Add the yolk.

4 Mix the melted butter, honey and sugar into the flour. Squeeze the mixture into a ball of dough.

To make Christmas decorations, thread narrow ribbons or gift tape through the holes in the cookies.

At Christmas time, German families get together for elaborate feasts. The table is laid with roasted meats, pasta, chestnuts, marzipan and fruit cakes.

5 Sprinkle flour onto a worktop and rolling pin. Roll out the dough until it is 1/4 in. thick.

6 Use cookie cutters to cut out different shapes. Roll out the leftover dough and cut out more shapes.

7 With a spatula, lift the cookies onto the baking sheet. Skewer a hole into the top of each one.

8 Bake the cookies for seven to eight minutes, until golden. Lift them onto a wire rack to cool.

9 Sift the powdered sugar into a bowl. Mix in the tablespoon of lemon juice, stirring really well.

10 If using food coloring, divide the icing into bowls. Mix a few drops of coloring into each bowl.

11 When the cookies are cool, spoon the icing into an icing bag. Squeeze the bag to pipe on the icing.

49

Austria

Austria is a small, central European country famous for its strudels, which are thin layers of pastry filled with fruit, poppyseeds or meat. Other specialties are cakes, dumplings, bread, noodles, smoked ham and Wiener schnitzel – slices of veal, fried in breadcrumbs.

Let the icing set before you cut the cake. It is traditionally served with freshly whipped cream.

Sachertorte

This famous chocolate cake is very rich. Known as 'Sacher's cake', it was first made by a chef called Franz Sacher, who baked it for an Austrian prince.

Ingredients

- 6 eggs
- ½ cup softened butter
- ½ cup sugar
- 8oz. semi-sweet chocolate
- ½ cup flour
- Two 8in. round cake pans, greased and lined with a circle of wax paper

For the filling and icing:
- 2 tablespoons butter
- 1 cup powdered sugar
- ½ cup apricot preserves
- 2 tablespoons cocoa powder

✷ Oven temperature: 325°F

1 Separate the eggs. Put the whites in one bowl and the yolks in another. Beat the yolks until smooth.

2 Beat the butter and sugar together until creamy. Stir in the egg yolks gradually.

3 Heat a saucepan of water over low heat. Break half the chocolate into a heatproof bowl.

4 Stand the bowl over the pan and stir the chocolate until it has melted. Stir it into the creamy butter mixture.

5 Whisk the egg whites in a large bowl until they are firm and form soft peaks when you lift the whisk. Use an electric mixer if needed.

6 Mix the flour into the cake mixture, then fold in the egg whites with a metal spoon, one spoonful at a time.

7 Divide the mixture into the cake pans. Smooth the top with the back of a spoon. Bake the cakes for 35 minutes.

8 Run a knife around the edge of the cakes to loosen them. Turn them out onto a wire rack and leave them to cool.

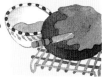

9 For a thick filling, melt the butter and the rest of the chocolate together in a bowl. Mix in a tablespoon of powdered sugar.

10 Spread the filling onto one half of the cake. Melt the preserves in a pan over low heat. Spread some of it over the filling.

11 Put the other half of the cake on top. Spread the rest of the preserves over the top and sides of the cake.

12 Sift the cocoa powder and the rest of the powdered sugar into a bowl. Add water a little at a time. Spread the icing all over the cake.

Coffee houses

Vienna is famous for its coffee houses, called Konditoreien. There you can drink different types of coffee, such as Einspänner, which has a ball of cream floating in it. They also serve all kinds of delicious cakes, tarts, pastries and strudels.

Fruit tarts

Viennese coffee houses serve a wide variety of coffees with elaborate toppings, such as frothy swirls of piped cream, sprinkled nuts, and wafer straws.

Switzerland

Switzerland lies in the middle of Europe. Its cooking is influenced by the countries around it, which include Italy, France and Germany, but there are also plenty of dishes that are uniquely Swiss. Many of these use fruits, potatoes or cheese.

Muesli

This healthy breakfast cereal was first invented by a Swiss doctor. It is a tasty mixture of grains, fruit and nuts. You can buy the old-fashioned oats at a supermarket. You'll need to start preparing muesli the night before you want to eat it.

Ingredients

- 3 tablespoons old-fashioned oats
- 6 tablespoons water
- 1 eating apple
- 2 teaspoons lemon juice
- 1 tablespoon raisins
- 1 tablespoon chopped mixed nuts
- 2 tablespoons milk
- 1 tablespoon honey

Muesli is delicious served with fresh, juicy berries.

1 At night, before you go to bed, put the oats into a bowl and pour the water on top.

2 In the morning, peel, halve, then grate the apple. Put it into a bowl, then stir the lemon juice into it.

3 Gently stir the apple into the softened oats. Add the nuts and raisins. Stir them in.

4 Put the muesli into a bowl. Pour on a little milk and drizzle some honey on top of each helping.

Raclette

Raclette is traditionally made by standing a block of cheese next to a fire, scraping the melted parts off with a knife, and eating them with potatoes, pickled onions and gherkins. In this recipe, the cheese is broiled. It's best to use Swiss Emmental or Gruyère cheese if you can.

Ingredients

- 4 medium potatoes
- 8oz. cheese
- a pinch of salt

1 Scrub the potatoes, but don't peel them. Cut out any eyes with the tip of a knife. Thinly slice the cheese.

Warming Emmental or Gruyère really brings out its flavor, so eat the potatoes while the cheese is still hot.

2 Put the potatoes in a pan of cold, salted water. Bring them to a boil and cook for 15 to 20 minutes.

3 See if the potatoes are cooked by pushing a sharp knife into one. It should go in and come out easily.

4 Drain the potatoes. Let them cool a little. Halve them. Lay cheese onto the cut side of each one.

5 Put the potatoes into a broiler. Broil them until the cheese melts and starts to bubble.

Cheese

There is a huge variety of cheeses around the world. Some are soft and creamy, while others are firmer, with a stronger flavor. Most cheeses are made from cows' milk, but some are made from goats' or sheep's milk.

Saint André – a cream cheese from France. It has a soft white rind and a mild flavor.

Emmental

Emmental and Gruyère – firm Swiss cheeses with a slightly sweet, nutty flavor.

Parmesan – a hard Italian cheese with a strong smell and flavor. It is grated over pasta or risotto, and cooked in many dishes.

Camembert – a cheese from France. It is creamy inside and has a soft rind on the outside.

Gruyère

Taleggio – a creamy, medium-soft Italian cheese with a mild flavor.

Edam

Gorgonzola – a creamy Italian blue cheese with a very strong flavor.

Halloumi – a mild cheese from Cyprus, made from cows', sheep's or goats' milk.

Gouda and Edam – mild, buttery Dutch cheeses with a thin rind and wax coating.

Gouda

Goats' cheese — can be mild and creamy, or firm with a strong taste. Some have a rind.

Cheddar — a British cheese with a full, rich flavor. It is often grated and used in cooked dishes.

Stilton — a creamy blue-veined English cheese made from cows' milk.

Smoked cheese — a mild German cheese with a smoky taste.

Feta — a crumbly Greek cheese with a strong, sharp flavor. It's used in salads with tomatoes and olives.

Manchego — a firm Spanish cheese with a strong flavor, made from sheep's milk.

Ricotta — a mild, low-fat Italian cheese often used for stuffing pasta, such as ravioli.

Cream cheese — smooth, buttery cheese often used as a spread or in cheesecakes.

Mozzarella — a soft Italian cheese with a mild flavor. It's often used as part of a pizza topping.

Roquefort — a blue-veined French cheese made from sheep's milk. It has a strong taste.

55

Hungary

Hungary is a central European country.
Hungarian summers are hot, but the winters
are bitterly cold. Many traditional dishes
are warming and spicy, using paprika, a hot
powder made from red peppers. Onions
and tomatoes are also used in lots of recipes.
Goulash is Hungary's most famous dish, but the
country is also known for its stuffed cabbage,
fish soups, and cottage cheese noodles.

Goulash

This spicy stew is flavored with sweet, fiery
paprika and served with dumplings. You
need to allow about two hours for it to cook.
This lets the meat become really tender.
To cook the goulash, you will need
a large pan with a lid.

Ingredients

- 1 large onion, peeled
- 1 clove of garlic
- 2 medium potatoes
- 2 tablespoons vegetable oil
- 1 ½lbs. stewing beef, cut into cubes
- 1 cup water
- 14oz. can chopped tomatoes
- 2 tablespoons paprika
- ½ teaspoon of salt
- a pinch of black pepper

For the dumplings:
- ½ cup all-purpose flour
- 3 teaspoons baking powder
- a large pinch of salt
- 2 tablespoons butter
- 1 egg
- about 1 tablespoon milk

To make paprika, the long, juicy red
peppers have to be dried and then
crushed and ground into a fine powder.

Dried
peppers

Powdered
paprika

1 Chop the onion finely. Peel and crush the garlic. Peel the potatoes and cut them into cubes.

2 Heat the oil in the large pan. Cook the onion and garlic over low heat until soft. Remove with a spoon.

3 Heat the remaining oil. Add the cubed meat and potatoes. Stir them until the meat is brown.

4 Add the onions, water, tomatoes, paprika, salt and pepper. Stir everything well and turn the heat to low.

5 Put the lid on the pan and cook the goulash over low heat for about two hours, until the meat is tender.

6 To make the dumplings, sift the flour into a mixing bowl. Add the baking powder and salt and mix them in.

7 Rub the butter into the flour. Break the egg and stir it in. Add enough milk to make a dough. Squeeze it together.

8 Roll the dough into small balls. Twenty minutes before serving, drop them into the pan and leave them to cook.

Sprinkle a little extra paprika over the goulash before you serve it. Goulash is traditionally eaten with noodles or rice.

Norway

Norway is one of the most northern countries in Europe, and has some of the world's most dramatic scenery. There are snow-capped mountains, deep sea inlets, and huge forests where many different berries grow. Winters in Norway are long and very cold, so the Norwegians preserve plenty of food to last them until spring. Meat and fish are often dried, smoked, or preserved with salt.

Many Norwegian forests are made up of evergreen trees, like these. Different types of berries grow there all year round.

Red fruit dessert

In summertime, many Norwegian people pick or buy berries. They use them to make special fruit desserts, like this one, to celebrate the short Scandinavian summer.

These red fruits are lingonberries. They grow wild in Norwegian forests and are often used in preserves, sauces and juices.

Ingredients

- 1lb. raspberries, blackcurrants or redcurrants, or a mixture of all three
- 2 tablespoons sugar
- 2 cups cold water
- 2 tablespoons cornstarch

1 Put the fruit, sugar and water in a pan. Cook over low heat until the fruit is soft. Let the fruit cool.

2 Use the back of a spoon to push it through a sieve into a bowl. Throw away any bits left in the sieve.

3 In a cup, mix a tablespoon of juices from the cooked fruit with the cornstarch, until smooth.

4 Stir the cornstarch mixture into the fruit. Then, pour the fruit back into the pan and bring it to a boil.

5 Turn the heat down low. Cook the fruit for five minutes, stirring it with a wooden spoon all the time.

6 Take the pan off the heat. Let the mixture cool. Pour it into some glasses or bowls. Chill them in a refrigerator.

Decorate the desserts with some fresh berries before you serve them.

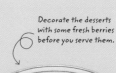

Strawberries

Blackberries

Blueberries

Raspberries

Redcurrants

Blackcurrants

Sweden

Sweden has huge expanses of forest where berries and mushrooms grow, and vast rivers, lakes and coastlines that are home to many kinds of fish, such as herring, eel and salmon.

Swedish food specialties are similar to those of other Scandinavian countries. They include meatballs, pâté, smoked meats and fish, and berry desserts. Traditional Swedish dishes can be served smörgåsbord-style, where diners pick and mix from a range of dishes laid out on a large table.

Dill

Parsley

Fresh parsley and dill are used to flavor and decorate many Swedish dishes.

Ingredients

- 1lb. potatoes
- 2 large onions, peeled
- ¼ cup butter
- 2 cans anchovies
- a pinch of salt and of pepper
- 1 cup milk

✳ Oven temperature: 400°F

Jansson's temptation

In Sweden, there are many stories about how this potato and anchovy recipe got its name. Some people think it was named after an opera singer, named Pelle Janzon. Others think it got its name from Erik Janson, a religious man from the 19th century. He had given up all wordly pleasures, but was tempted into eating this delicious concoction. To make this recipe, you'll need a large, heatproof dish.

When the dish is cooked, the top layer of potatoes turns crisp golden brown.

In Sweden, anchovies are kept fresh in ice before being canned in a sugar and spice brine.

1 Peel the potatoes. Cut them into thin strips about 2in. long. Put them into a bowl of cold water.

2 Peel the onions, chop them finely, then fry them gently in half of the butter until they are soft.

3 Drain the potatoes in a colander. Put a layer of them into a large, heatproof dish. Drain and wash the anchovies.

4 Cover the potatoes with a layer of anchovies. Cover the anchovies with a layer of the softened onions.

5 Repeat the layers of potato, anchovies and onion, finishing with a layer of potato.

6 Add the salt and pepper. Pour the milk all over the top. It will sink to the bottom of the dish.

7 Cut the rest of the butter into small pieces and dot them around the dish. Bake it for about 45 minutes.

61

Denmark

Denmark is a southern Scandinavian country. It's made up of a peninsula and more than 400 smaller islands. The climate is warm in summer and cold and wet in winter. Denmark has rich farmlands which produce bacon, pork and a wide variety of cheeses.

Shrimp and lemon — put a lettuce leaf onto the bread. Spoon shrimp on top and add some black pepper and a twist of lemon.

Smørrebrød

Smørrebrød are open sandwiches. They can be made with any ingredients and are usually eaten with a knife and fork. The best bread to use is dark rye bread. To make the sandwiches, butter the bread then lay the ingredients on top.

Salami and tomato — cover the bread with slices of salami. Add slices of tomato and some red onion.

Preparing ingredients

LETTUCE

Cut off the lettuce stalk. Tear off and wash as many leaves as you need. Dry them on a paper towel.

ONIONS

Peel an onion and cut off the ends. Slice the onion finely, then separate the slices to make onion rings.

EGGS

1 To hard-boil eggs, heat some water in a pan until it bubbles. Then, boil the eggs for ten minutes.

2 Put the eggs into a bowl of cold water. Tap each egg on the edge of the bowl to crack the shell. Peel it off.

Fish

Salmon and herring are used in lots of Danish dishes and are prepared in many different ways. For example, gravlax is raw salmon that has been soaked in a mixture of salt, sugar and dill.

For centuries, this Danish harbor in Copenhagen was a fishing port. Today, most of the boats are for tours, but the harbor is home to many seafood restaurants.

Blue cheese and lettuce — cover the bread with lettuce and slices of cheese. Sprinkle cress on top.

Cheese and tomato — lay thin slices of cheese on the bread. Then, lay a row of sliced tomato along the middle. Add a gherkin garnish.

Smoked salmon and egg — cover the bread with slices of hard-boiled egg and smoked salmon. Sprinkle it with chopped dill.

Cress and herring — lay hard-boiled egg slices and a fillet of pickled herring on the bread. Sprinkle it with cress.

Garnishes

LEMONS

Halve a slice of lemon. Make a cut in the middle of each half. Twist the ends so that the slice stands up.

GHERKINS

Make thin cuts along the length of a gherkin, cutting almost to the end. Spread the slices out like a fan.

Russia

Russia spans Asia and Europe. It is very cold in the winter, so root vegetables, such as potatoes, beetroot and turnips grow well there. In the summer, farmers grow wheat and other grains on the Russian steppes, the huge grasslands in the middle of the country. Russian specialties include blinis, which are small pancakes made from buckwheat flour, and borscht, a red soup made from beetroot and sour cream.

Wheat grows well in central and southern Russia. Farmers grow enough wheat to feed the Russian population and to export worldwide.

Beef stroganoff

Adding sour cream to meat is common in Russian cooking, but this quick and tasty recipe for beef stroganoff uses expensive steak, so it is usually only made on special occasions. It is said to have been created in the 1700s for a Russian Count, named Alexander Stroganoff.

Serve the stroganoff hot with egg noodles or boiled rice.

1 Wipe the mushrooms clean, then slice them. Cut the ends off the onion and peel it, then slice it thinly.

2 Cut the steak into narrow strips about 2½in. long. Sprinkle them with a little salt and pepper.

Ingredients

- 4oz. mushrooms
- 1 medium onion
- 1lb. rump or fillet steak
- salt and black pepper
- 2 tablespoons butter
- 1 teaspoon dijon mustard
- ½ cup sour cream

3 Melt the butter in a frying pan. Fry the onion slices over low heat until soft, stirring all the time.

4 Add the mushrooms to the pan, stir them in and cook them for two minutes. Stir in the mustard.

5 Add the steak. Stir the mixture for about five minutes, until the meat is brown on both sides.

6 Turn the heat down and stir in the sour cream. Cook the stroganoff gently for two minutes more, then serve.

A Russian delicacy

Caviar is one of the most well-known luxury foods, and is made from the eggs of certain fish, such as sturgeon and salmon. The eggs are preserved in salt, giving them a sharp, tangy taste. They are usually served as a starter.

Caviar can be very pricey. There are many different types. Some of the best and most expensive ones come from Russia, and are collected from Beluga sturgeons, which are found in Russian waters.

This red caviar is from Russian salmon. Caviar from sturgeons is more expensive and ranges in color from black and dark brown to amber or white.

Bread

In parts of the world where wheat and other grains grow, people have been baking bread for thousands of years. A lot of bread is made from wheat flour, but rye, barley, oats or maize (corn) can also be made into bread. Some breads have yeast or other ingredients added to them to make them rise, but others are flat breads.

In Egypt, many bakers make a traditional type of flat bread, shaping it into circles by hand before putting it into a wood-fired oven.

Croissants — flaky crescents of bread layered with butter. They are often eaten for breakfast in France.

Brioche — a sweet French bread made as a loaf or as buns.

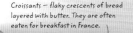

Pretzels — German bread shapes, covered in salt. They are also popular in America.

Challah — a rich bread, usually braided, which is traditionally made for Jewish holy days.

Bagels — soft bread rings with a chewy crust. Bagels are a Jewish specialty.

Sourdough rye bread — a heavy bread popular in Russia and much of Eastern Europe.

Baguette — a French stick of bread with a soft inside, and a crispy crust.

Barbari — a North African flat bread.

Hard dough bread — a Caribbean bread, made with soy flour.

Pita bread — a Middle Eastern flat bread that can be split and filled.

Farmhouse loaf — a soft, white British loaf with a thick crust.

Naan — an Indian flat bread.

Dark rye bread — eaten in Germany and many Eastern European countries.

Focaccia — an Italian bread that is often flavored with olives, garlic or herbs and sprinkled with crushed salt.

Soda bread — traditional Irish bread, usually made with brown flour.

Greece

Greece lies in southern Europe, on the Mediterranean Sea. Much of Greece is mountainous and the land is rocky and bare, but olive and lemon trees grow well there, and sheep and goats graze the hills.

Well-known Greek dishes include avgolemono, an egg and lemon soup, and spanakopita, a type of spinach pie. Greece is also famous for tzatziki, a yogurt, garlic and cucumber mixture, which is often eaten as a starter with pita bread.

Eggplants grow hanging down from tall vines. They're very sensitive to cold, so grow well in warm countries, such as Greece.

Ingredients

- 4 tablespoons butter
- 2 tablespoons all-purpose flour
- 2½ cups milk
- a pinch of ground nutmeg
- 1 large eggplant
- 1 large onion
- 1 clove of garlic
- 4 tablespoons oil
- 1lb. ground lamb or beef

- 14oz. can tomatoes
- 2 tablespoons tomato purée
- 1 teaspoon ground cinnamon
- a pinch of salt and of black pepper
- 2 eggs
- 4 tablespoons grated Cheddar cheese

✱ Oven temperature: 375°F

Moussaka

This Greek eggplant dish has a creamy topping. It is traditionally made with lamb but people sometimes use other meat. You'll need an ovenproof casserole dish.

1 Melt the butter in a pan. Stir in the flour to make a smooth paste. Cook it gently for a minute, stirring well.

2 Take the pan off the heat and stir in the milk. Add the nutmeg. Heat the sauce until it boils. Set it aside to cool.

3 Turn on the oven. Cut the eggplant into thin slices. Peel and chop the onion, and peel and crush the clove of garlic.

4 Heat two tablespoons of the oil in a pan that has a lid. Fry the onions and garlic gently, until they are soft.

5 Add the ground meat, breaking it up with a spoon. Fry it, stirring well until it is brown all over.

6 Stir in the tomatoes, tomato purée, cinnamon, salt and pepper. Cover and cook gently for 20 minutes.

7 Heat the rest of the oil in a frying pan. Fry the eggplant until it is soft. Add more oil if needed.

8 Spoon half the meat mixture into the bottom of a casserole dish. Cover it with a layer of the sliced eggplant.

9 Repeat the layers, finishing with a layer of eggplant. Break the eggs into a bowl and beat them. Stir them into the sauce.

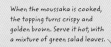

10 Pour the sauce over the moussaka. Sprinkle it with grated cheese and bake it in the oven for 45 minutes.

When the moussaka is cooked, the topping turns crispy and golden brown. Serve it hot, with a mixture of green salad leaves.

Turkey

Turkey lies at the eastern end of the Mediterranean Sea. Some of the country is in Europe, and most is in Asia, so it has always been influenced by the cooking of both continents.

Popular Turkish dishes include rice dishes called pilaffs, stuffed vegetables, milk puddings flavored with orange blossom or rosewater, and deliciously sweet, nutty pastries. Grilled or baked fish is also a common dish.

Rosemary   Oregano   Lemon

Ingredients

- 1½lbs. lamb or skinless, boneless chicken breasts
- 4 tablespoons lemon juice
- 4 tablespoons olive oil
- ½ teaspoon dried or fresh chopped oregano
- a large pinch of salt and of black pepper
- 8 lettuce leaves, washed
- half a cucumber
- 4 tomatoes
- ½ teaspoon dried or fresh chopped rosemary
- 8 pita breads

- 8 metal or wooden skewers

Shish kebabs

Shish kebabs are cubes of meat cooked on a skewer. You can use metal or wooden skewers to make them. If you use wooden skewers, soak them in water for 30 minutes first, to stop them from burning. You'll need to allow an hour for soaking the meat in a sauce before you cook it, to make it more tender.

You can serve the kebabs with long-grain rice instead of pita bread, if you prefer.

1 Wash the meat and put it on a chopping board. Carefully cut it into cubes about 1in. across.

2 Mix three tablespoons of lemon juice, the olive oil, the oregano and salt and pepper in a bowl.

3 Stir the meat into the bowl. Cover the bowl with foodwrap. Leave it in the refrigerator for an hour.

4 Cut the lettuce into strips. Chop the cucumber into small pieces and cut the tomatoes into quarters.

5 Push six meat cubes onto each skewer, leaving gaps between them. Sprinkle with rosemary.

6 Turn on the grill. Cook the kebabs for 10-12 minutes. Turn them every so often so they brown all over.

7 Turn down the grill and toast the pita breads for a minute or two. Then, slice each one along the top.

8 Fill each pita bread with some salad and the meat from one kebab. Sprinkle with a little more lemon juice.

Kebabs

The word "kebab" originally meant "fried meat" in Arabic, but now is a general term for a dish that includes pieces of meat that have been grilled, roasted or fried.

Shish kebabs use cubes of meat but, for some other types of kebab, the meat is ground, then squeezed around a skewer and grilled, or shaped into balls and fried. Doner kebabs are slices of meat that have been slowly roasted on a tall, vertical skewer. They're often served in bread.

These skewers are rotating slowly, grilling the meat evenly as they turn. The cooked parts of the meat will be cut off in very thin slices.

The Middle East

Dried dates

The area called the Middle East is very warm and dry. It stretches from North Africa across to southern Russia. The Middle East includes many countries, races and religions. Despite their differences, all the countries have similar ways of preparing food.

Common ingredients

Middle Eastern cooking tends to use a lot of wheat, spices and dates. Various forms of wheat appear in both savory and sweet dishes; spices add flavor and color to the food, and dates are used in many desserts to add a sticky sweetness.

These spices are commonly used in Middle Eastern cooking to add different flavors. Paprika and curry powder are hot, sumak is sour, and saffron is bitter.

Date palm trees, like these, grow throughout the Middle East. The dates grow in huge clusters at the bottom of the large leaves.

Tabbouleh

This salad comes from Lebanon, on the eastern side of the Mediterranean Sea. It is made with chopped herbs, fresh vegetables, and a grain called cracked wheat. All the ingredients are tossed in a delicious lemony dressing.

Ingredients

- 1 cup cracked wheat
- 4 tablespoons parsley
- 2 tablespoons fresh mint
- 3 tomatoes
- half a cucumber
- 6 green onions

- 8 lettuce leaves

For the dressing:
- 2 lemons
- 6 tablespoons olive oil
- salt and black pepper

1 Put the cracked wheat in a bowl and cover it with boiling water. Leave it to soak for about 20 minutes.

2 Chop the parsley, mint, tomatoes and cucumber finely. Trim the ends off the green onions and slice them.

3 When the wheat is soft, pour it into a sieve. Press it with the back of a spoon to squeeze out excess water.

4 Wash the lettuce leaves and pat them dry. Cut the lemons in half and squeeze out the juice.

5 For the dressing, mix the olive oil, six tablespoons of lemon juice, and a pinch of salt and of black pepper.

6 Put the wheat into a bowl. Mix in all the other chopped ingredients. Pour on the dressing and mix it in well.

To serve, put two lettuce leaves on each person's plate and spoon some tabbouleh on top.

Hummus

Creamy dips are a popular starter or "mezze" in the Middle East, Greece and Turkey. They are made from different things, such as fish or eggplants. Hummus is a garlicky dip made from chickpeas and tahini (or tahina), a thick sesame seed paste. You can buy tahini in some supermarkets and health food stores.

Ingredients

- 14oz. can chickpeas
- 1 clove of garlic
- 2 lemons
- 2 tablespoons olive oil
- 1 tablespoon light tahini paste
- a pinch of salt and of black pepper

To serve:
- 1 tablespoon finely chopped parsley
- paprika

1 Open the can of chickpeas and drain them into a colander. Shake it gently to get rid of any excess liquid.

2 Put the chickpeas into a blender if you have one, or push them through a sieve with a spoon, to make a paste.

3 Peel the clove of garlic, then crush it into a paste. Cut the lemons in half and squeeze the juice out.

4 Mix six tablespoons of lemon juice, the garlic, oil, tahini, and salt and pepper into the chickpea paste.

Sprinkle the hummus with chopped parsley and paprika. Serve it with warmed pita bread and some olives.

Chickpeas

Chickpeas, also known as garbanzo beans or ceci beans, are used in many Middle Eastern dishes. They are also used in recipes in some Mediterranean countries and India. Chickpeas grow in pods about 1 inch long, with only one or two chickpeas growing in each pod. They are light brown, slightly larger than peas and have a mild nutty taste.

Fruit salad

This refreshing, sweet salad is served as a light snack or dessert in many Middle Eastern countries. It's especially popular during the month of Ramadan, when Muslims can only eat or drink while the Sun is down.

Ingredients

- 3 large oranges, peeled
- 1 peach
- ½ melon, peeled
- 5 fresh figs
- 5 dates
- 3 tablespoons rosewater
- a handful of pomegranate seeds
- ½ teaspoon cinnamon
- ½ teaspoon powdered sugar

To give the fruit salad an extra chewy texture and sweet flavor, you can sprinkle a few raisins over the top.

1 Cut the rind and pith off the oranges. Slice them and the peach, too. Slice the melon, then cut the slices into chunks.

2 Chop the figs into pieces. Cut the dates lengthways, then take the pits out. Chop the dates into pieces.

3 Arrange the pieces of orange, peach and melon on a plate. Scatter the chopped dates and figs over them.

4 Sprinkle rosewater and pomegranate seeds over the salad. Sift the cinnamon and powdered sugar over the top.

Cakes and pastries

Many countries have their own traditional cakes, pastries and cookies. The recipes are usually based on local ingredients and many are baked for special occasions.

Macaroons — small, sweet cookies made from ground almonds and egg whites. The most famous macaroons are Italian amaretti.

Carrot cake — a sweet American cake made with grated carrots. It is topped with cream cheese icing.

Pecan pie — traditionally from the Southern states of America. It has a sweet, crunchy pecan nut filling and is often served with whipped cream.

American muffins — sweet, light, small cakes, often flavored with fruit or chocolate.

Indian cakes — these are really candy rather than cakes. They tend to be very sweet. Jalebi, for example are deep-fried rings of batter soaked in syrup.

Profiteroles — small buns of choux pastry originally from France. They are topped with chocolate and filled with cream. Chocolate éclairs taste the same, but are a different shape.

Panettone — a spicy Italian fruit bread traditionally eaten at Christmas. It is usually sold in big decorated boxes.

Fruit tarts — little tarts with a pastry base, sometimes filled with custard. They are popular in European pâtisseries.

Panforte — a rich, dense, spicy cake from Siena in Italy. It is usually cut into small slices and eaten with coffee.

Baklava — very sweet cake popular in Greece and the Middle East. It's made of wafer-thin filo pastry filled with nuts and soaked in honey.

Konafa (kadeifi) — a syrupy sweet Middle Eastern cake made from pastry that looks a little like fine spaghetti. You can buy the pastry ready-made in Greek and Turkish shops.

Chinese cakes — tend to be very sweet. Moon cakes are traditionally made to celebrate a mid-fall festival.

India

India is a country of contrasts, ranging from the Himalayan mountains to steamy rainforests and hot, dry plains. Each region has its own special dishes, and these are often influenced by different religions. Indian food has a distinctive taste because of the unique mixtures of spices and flavorings that Indian cooks use.

Basmati rice

Thousands of people visit street markets, like this one, every day to buy locally grown fruit and vegetables. Rice and meat are usually sold indoors.

Basmati

The best rice for Indian cooking is Basmati rice. To stop the grains from sticking together, soak the rice in cold water for 30 minutes first, then follow the cooking instructions on the package.

In some parts of India, entire meals are eaten from banana leaves, like this.

Bhuna gosht

This is a spicy lamb dish. For a filling meal, serve it with rice, dhal (lentil stew) and raita (a yogurt and cucumber dish). The recipes for dhal and raita are on page 80.

Ingredients

- 1 onion
- 2 cloves of garlic
- 1in. piece ginger, peeled
- 3 medium tomatoes
- 1½lbs. lean lamb
- a pinch of salt
- ½ teaspoon chili powder
- 1 teaspoon paprika
- 2 teaspoons ground cilantro
- 1 teaspoon ground cumin
- 1 teaspoon turmeric
- 4 tablespoons butter
- ½ cup water
- 1 teaspoon black pepper
- 4 tablespoons lemon juice

Put the bhuna gosht into a warm dish, as it's at its best when hot. You can serve it with rice or naan bread.

1 Peel and chop the onion. Peel and crush the garlic. Grate the ginger. Cut the tomatoes into quarters.

2 Cut the lamb into cubes. Put it into a bowl. Mix the salt, garlic, ginger and spices into the lamb.

3 Melt the butter in a saucepan over a medium heat. Stir in the onion and lamb. When the onions turn brown, add the water.

4 Leave the pan on low heat for around 10 minutes. Then, if the water has gone, add a little more.

5 Turn the heat up to medium. Let the bhuna simmer for 25-30 minutes, stirring it from time to time.

6 Add the pepper, lemon juice and tomatoes. Stir it continuously for another five minutes, then serve.

Dhal

Dhal (dal) is an Indian word for all pulses, such as dried beans, split peas and lentils. Pulses form the main part of many meals in India, because lots of people are vegetarian. This is a recipe for a thick, spicy lentil stew, which is also called dhal.

Lentils

Ingredients

- 1 clove of garlic
- 1 small onion
- 4oz. red lentils
- 4 tablespoons butter
- a pinch of chili powder
- 1 teaspoon turmeric
- 1 teaspoon ground cumin
- 2½ cups water
- a pinch of salt

1   Peel and crush the garlic clove. Peel the onion and chop it finely. Then, rinse the lentils in a sieve.

2   Melt the butter in a deep pan. Gently cook the garlic and onion for three to five minutes until they are soft.

3   Add the chili powder, turmeric, cumin, lentils and water. Bring the mixture to a boil, stirring all the time.

4   Turn the heat down and let the mixture simmer for about 20 minutes until the lentils are soft.

5   Take the pan off the heat and add the salt. Beat the mixture well with a wooden spoon until it's nearly smooth.

Cucumber raita

Raita is made of natural yogurt mixed with fresh vegetables, herbs and sometimes nuts. It's served with spicy dishes to provide a contrasting taste and to cool your mouth down.

Ingredients

- a handful fresh mint leaves
- half a cucumber
- 1 cup (9½ oz.) plain yogurt
- a pinch of salt and of black pepper

1   Wash the mint leaves. Shake them dry. Strip the leafy part away from their stalks, then chop the leaves finely.

2   Peel the green skin off the cucumber, then cut it into slices lengthways. Cut the slices into small strips.

3   Whisk the yogurt in a bowl until it is smooth. Stir in the cucumber and mint and season with salt and pepper.

Contrasting flavors

A typical Indian meal is made up of several dishes with contrasting savory, sweet and spicy flavors, colors and textures. There is usually a meat dish, a dhal, a vegetable dish, rice, a raita and maybe fresh mango or lime chutney and bread, such as a puri or chapatti.

The food is sometimes served in small metal bowls called katoris. These are often put on a large tray called a thali, and meals like this are called thalis too.

Cucumber raita

Bhuna gosht

Basmati rice

Dhal

Thailand

Cilantro

For centuries, Thailand, in Southeast Asia, has been a center for international trade. Thai cooking is a blend of Asian and European influences. Portuguese traders brought chilies, Indians provided curries and spices, and the Chinese taught Thai cooks how to stir-fry.

Chicken in coconut sauce

Coconut adds a creamy taste in this typical Thai dish. You can also taste the blend of garlic, chili powder and ground ginger.

In floating markets, a wide variety of tropical fruits, flowers and other fresh produce is sold from boats.

Ingredients

For the curry:
- 4 skinless, boneless chicken breasts, washed
- 2 tablespoons canola oil
- 1½ cups coconut milk
- 7oz. sugarsnap peas
- juice of 1 lime
- fresh basil or Thai basil leaves to garnish

For the paste (or you can buy green curry paste – see its package for instructions on how to use it):
- 4 shallots
- 2 cloves of garlic, peeled
- ½ teaspoon ground cumin
- ¼–½ teaspoon chili flakes (depending on how hot you want it)
- ½ teaspoon ground cilantro
- a pinch of salt and of black pepper
- 1in. piece fresh root ginger
- a handful of fresh cilantro
- 2 tablespoons fish sauce
- 2 stalks lemon grass

These coconuts have been shelled and shaped for people to drink from.

Serve the chicken with boiled or spiced rice.

1 Trim any fat off the chicken. Cut the chicken into strips. Heat a tablespoon of oil in a large frying pan over medium heat for 20 seconds.

2 Add the chicken to the pan. Stir it for five minutes. When it starts to turn golden, take it out of the pan and set it aside.

3 Cut the ends off the shallots. Peel them. Chop them into pieces. Heat a tablespoon of oil in a large saucepan for 20 seconds.

4 Add the shallots to the pan. Crush the garlic. Add it, the cumin, chili flakes, ground cilantro, and salt and pepper to the pan.

5 Cook over medium heat, stirring occasionally until the shallots are soft. Peel and grate the ginger. Add it to the pan.

6 Chop the fresh cilantro into small pieces. Add it and the fish sauce to the pan. Peel off the outer layer of the lemon grass.

7 Cut the stalks in half lengthways. Use a rolling pin to roll over each half. Add them and the coconut milk to the pan. Bring to a boil.

8 Let the mixture simmer for five minutes. Add the chicken. Cook for five minutes. Lift out the pieces of lemon grass.

9 Add the sugarsnap peas. Cook for another five minutes. Squeeze lime juice over it. Chop the basil leaves and sprinkle them on top.

83

Spices

The rich flavors of Indian, Thai and Indonesian food come from the many different spices cooks use. A dish can contain just one spice or as many as fifteen. Each spice has its own distinctive flavor. Spices can come from dried roots, bark, seeds, berries and other fruit.

Turmeric — dyes food yellow and has a strong, slightly bitter flavor.

Mustard seeds — give food a delicious nutty flavor when it's cooked in mustard seed oil.

Cilantro seeds — have a delicate flavor and are usually ground.

Cumin seeds — have an earthy flavor and are used a lot in Indian cooking.

Lemon grass — lemony-flavored stems used to flavor dishes, such as rice.

Kaffir lime leaves — have a spicy lime flavor and are added to many Thai and Indonesian dishes. They're removed at the end of cooking.

Fresh ginger — a knobbed brown "root." It is peeled, then grated.

Nutmeg — is grated into a powder. It's used to add flavor to savory Asian dishes.

Whole cloves — used in rice and meat dishes, they have a strong flavor.

Many spices are dried before they are used. In some places, they are spread out to dry in the sun but, in others, they're dried in huge ovens.

Chili powder and red chilies — give food a hot, fiery flavor.

Cardamom pods — sweetly flavored dried seed pods used either whole or ground in both sweet and savory dishes. Sometimes just the seeds are used.

Garlic — each head of garlic is made up of individual cloves.

Cinnamon — the dried inner bark of a tropical tree. The sticks are used whole in meat and rice dishes, and are not eaten. Ground cinnamon is often used to flavor cakes and cookies.

Cinnamon sticks and powder

In Eastern spice markets, like this one in Istanbul in Turkey, spices are usually heaped into sacks and sold loose by weight.

Preparing spices

Indian, Thai and Indonesian cooks usually buy spices whole, then roast them or grind them when they're needed. This way, the spices stay fresh and keep their flavor.

ROASTING

1 Heat a frying pan over medium heat. Add the spices and cook them for about two minutes.

2 Shake the pan to roast the spices evenly, and stop them from sticking. Take them off the heat when they turn darker.

GRINDING

1 To grind whole spices, put them into a deep bowl, called a mortar. Use the pestle to crush them into a fine powder.

China

China is a vast country and the dishes vary from one region to another. They include lots of fish and seafood in the south, whereas in the north, people more often eat meat. In the central regions the food is spicy and contains garlic and chilies. The main dish in most Chinese meals is usually eaten with rice or noodles.

Ginger

Mushrooms

Green onions

Ingredients

- 1 tablespoon butter
- 1 cup long grain rice
- ⅔ cup water
- ½ teaspoon salt
- 12 mushrooms
- ¼ small head of Chinese cabbage
- 6 green onions
- 1 clove of garlic
- 1in. cube fresh root ginger
- 2 tablespoons canola oil
- 4oz. frozen peas
- 5oz. bean sprouts
- 3 tablespoons dark soy sauce

Fried rice with vegetables

Lots of Chinese cooking is stir-fried. All the ingredients are cut up into small pieces about the same size, then cooked quickly in a large pan over high heat.

Rice is one of China's main crops. It is grown in huge paddy fields, like these, which are flooded with water to help the rice grow.

1 Melt the butter in a pan over low heat. Stir in the rice and cook it for a few minutes until it becomes transparent.

2 Add the water and salt, then put a lid on the pan. Cook the rice gently for 15 minutes without stirring it.

3 The rice is cooked when it is tender and has absorbed all the water. Bite a few grains to see if they're done.

4 Wipe the mushrooms and slice them. Slice the cabbage leaves into strips. Cut the green onions into 1in. slices.

5 Peel and crush the clove of garlic. Peel the ginger and grate it using the large holes of a cheese grater.

6 Heat the canola oil in a frying pan until hot. Fry the garlic and ginger for 30 seconds, stirring all the time.

7 Add the mushrooms and cook them over a high heat for another two minutes, still stirring. Stir in the green onions.

8 Add the peas, rice, cabbage leaves and bean sprouts. Stir everything over a high heat for about five minutes.

9 When the vegetables are just tender, sprinkle the soy sauce over them and stir-fry them for another two minutes.

It's a good idea to serve the stir-fried rice in a warmed serving dish, as it's best while still hot.

Sweet and sour spare ribs

Chinese dishes often combine flavors that are quite different from each other. You will need to start preparing this recipe about one hour and 20 minutes before eating it, as the meat has to soak in a sauce for an hour.

Soy sauce

Soy sauce is a salty sauce used to add flavor, and sometimes color, to Chinese cooking. It is made from soy beans, wheat flour, water and salt. Soy sauce is added to cooked dishes, such as stir-fries, and is often used in a marinade, a sauce that meat is soaked in, to make it more tender.

Ingredients

- 1½lbs. pork spare ribs
- ½ teaspoon salt
- 2 tablespoons sugar
- 1 tablespoon light soy sauce
- 2 tablespoons wine vinegar
- 1½ tablespoons tomato purée
- 2 tablespoons orange juice
- 1 small onion
- 1in. cube fresh ginger
- 1 clove of garlic
- 2 tablespoons vegetable oil

You can serve the ribs with boiled rice and a small bowl of soy sauce.

1 Rinse the spare ribs and pat them dry with a paper towel. Cut off as much of the fat as you can. Sprinkle with salt.

2 Pour the sugar, soy sauce, vinegar, tomato purée and orange juice into a deep casserole dish and stir them well.

3 Put the ribs into the sauce and cover them with plastic foodwrap. Leave them in the refrigerator for an hour.

4 Peel the onion and chop it finely. Peel the ginger and grate it using the small holes of a grater. Peel and crush the garlic.

5 Heat half of the oil in a large frying pan. Fry the onion, ginger and garlic until the onion is soft, then remove them from the pan.

6 Add the rest of the oil to the pan. Fry the ribs over high heat for about five minutes, turning them over halfway through.

7 Turn the heat down a little. Add the onion, garlic and ginger. Pour the sauce from the casserole dish over the top.

8 Cook for about 10 more minutes until the ribs are cooked, stirring them all the time so they don't burn.

Using chopsticks

Chinese food is usually eaten with chopsticks, made from wood, bamboo or plastic. Eating with chopsticks can be quite tricky, so you might need to practice holding them first.

Let the bottom one touch your third finger.

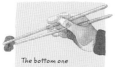

The bottom one should stay still.

1 Hold the top chopstick between your first two fingers. Rest the bottom one in the 'v' between your finger and thumb.

2 Move your first finger to make the top chopstick move up and down. The ends will pinch together to pick up food.

Chopsticks come in a variety of lengths, weights and materials. These women have the easiest ones to use, which are wooden, short, and of medium weight.

Japan

Japan is made up of four main islands to the east of mainland Asia. The Japanese eat a lot of light and low-fat food, such as fish, seafood, vegetables, noodles and rice. It is often served raw or only lightly cooked and is some of the healthiest food in the world.

These Japanese pickles, called tsukemono, are served with rice. There are hundreds of varieties made from all sorts of vegetables, fruits, fish and meat.

Sushi

Sushi is bite-sized parcels of vinegar-soaked rice topped with raw fish, seafood or vegetables. This popular snack is often wrapped in sheets of dried seaweed and accompanied by pickled vegetables. In Japan, you can buy takeout sushi from cafés called sushi bars.

Sushi is often eaten with flakes of pickled ginger.

Vegetable casserole

Japanese food can be spiced up by dipping the pieces into a strong sauce.

Dishes that have sauces or gravy are served with long-grain rice.

Vegetable casserole

This is a traditional winter dish in Japan, cooked in a casserole dish with a lid. It's usually served with rice or noodles and a tangy dipping sauce. Dip each vegetable into the sauce before you eat it.

1 Peel the carrots and trim off the ends. Cut them in half, then in half lengthways. Slice each piece into thin strips.

2 Trim off both ends of the green onions. Then, cut them into pieces about 1in. long, cutting them at a slant.

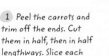

3 Wipe the mushrooms clean. Then, trim the stems and cut a cross in the top of each one. Turn on the oven.

4 Roll each cabbage leaf into a sausage shape. Slice across each one. This will make thin strips when they unroll.

5 Take the tofu out of its package and cut it carefully into cubes. Make the cubes about 1in. across.

6 Stir the bouillon cube and boiling water together in a measuring cup. Add the soy sauce, brown sugar and salt.

7 Boil the noodles following the instructions on their package. Arrange the vegetables and noodles in the dish.

8 Pour the broth over everything, then put the lid on the dish. Bake the casserole for about 45 minutes.

9 To make the dipping sauce, cut the lemons in half and squeeze them. Put six tablespoons of the juice into a bowl.

10 Mix the soy sauce and brown sugar into the lemon juice. Then, put the sauce into the refrigerator to chill.

Australia

The landscape of Australia is spectacular and varied, from dry bushlands and scrubby deserts in the central Outback regions, to lush rainforests in the north where exotic fruits grow. There are fine white beaches and deep blue bays teeming with fish and seafood, and vast areas of farmland, where cows and sheep are reared, and grain, fruit and vegetables are grown. Australian cooking uses local ingredients, but also has a lot of European, Asian, Chinese and Japanese influences.

Ingredients

For the meringues:
- 2 large eggs, at room temperature
- 1 cup powdered sugar

For the topping:
- ½ cup heavy cream
- ½ teaspoon vanilla
- 1 kiwi
- 1 passion fruit

- 2 baking sheets

✷ Oven temperature: 225°F

Mini pavlovas

This popular dessert is named after a famous ballerina, Anna Pavlova. During a trip to Australia in the 1920s, this light and airy dish was created especially for her.

Passion fruit

1 Lay two baking sheets on baking parchment and draw around them. Cut out the shapes and lay them in the sheets.

2 Turn on the oven. Separate the white from the yolk for each egg. Put the whites into a bowl. You don't need the yolks.

3 Whisk the egg whites until they are very thick, making stiff peaks when you lift the whisk up. You can use an electric mixer.

4 Whisk a teaspoon of the sugar into the egg whites. Keep whisking in spoonfuls of sugar until all the sugar has been added.

5 Scoop up a spoonful of the meringue mixture with a tablespoon. Use another spoon to push it onto one of the trays.

6 Use the back of a spoon to flatten the top of the meringue dollop. Make more dollops, leaving spaces between them.

7 Put the meringues in the oven. After 40 minutes, turn off the oven. Leave them inside. After 15 minutes, carefully lift them out.

8 Leave the meringues to cool. Meanwhile, pour the cream and vanilla into a bowl. Whisk them strongly until the mixture is thick.

9 Peel the kiwi. Chop it into pieces. When the meringues are cold, spoon cream over each one. Put kiwi pieces in the cream.

10 Halve the passion fruit. Scoop out some of the juice from inside with a spoon. Pour the juice over the pavlovas.

Pavlovas were inspired by the shape and color of the tutu Anna Pavlova wore to perform the ballet "Swan Lake" during her tour of Australia.

Usborne Quicklinks

The *Usborne Quicklinks Website* is packed with links to all the best websites on the internet. For downloadable recipes and links to over 100 recommended websites for this book, go to **www.usborne-quicklinks.com** and enter the keywords: **world cookbook**

There you will find links to websites where you can:
· Watch movies of different dishes being prepared
· Play food games online
· Take culinary quizzes
· Find out about different cultures all over the world

Internet safety

When using the internet, make sure you follow these internet safety guidelines which are also displayed on the *Usborne Quicklinks Website*.

· Children should ask their parent's or guardian's permission before using the internet.

· Never give details of your full name, address, telephone number or school, or any other personal information.

· If a website asks you to log in or register by typing your name or email address, children should ask an adult's permission first.

For more on using the internet safely and securely, see the **Net Help** area on the **Usborne Quicklinks Website**.

Acknowledgements

Additional designs by Nelupa Hussain
Food stylists: Eliza Baird, Bethany Heald and Dagmar Vesely
Additional illustrations by Antonia Miller
Digital manipulation: Keith Furnival
Americanization: Carrie Armstrong

With thanks also to Fiona Patchett, Catherine Atkinson
and Abigail Wheatley for helping to perfect the recipes

Every effort has been made to trace the copyright holders of the material in this book.
If any rights have been omitted, the publishers offer to rectify this in any subsequent
edition, following notification. The publishers are grateful to the following organizations
and individuals for their contributions and permission to reproduce material:

p.6 Pretzels © foodfolio/Alamy; **p.6** New York delicatessen © Robert Holmes/CORBIS; **p9** Pumpkin
pie © Acme Food Arts; **p9** Pumpkins © inga spence/Alamy; **p.10** Maple trees © Gaertner/Alamy; **p.10** Collecting
sap © icpix_can/Alamy; **p.12** Mexican wraps © Matthew Mawson/Alamy; **p.18** Palm tree
© Tetra Images/Getty Images; **p.18** Mangoes © Pulsar Imagens/Delfim Matins/Getty Images; **p.21** Banana tree
© Caro/Alamy; **p.22** Stuffed peppers © Art of Food/Alamy; **p.25** Family making flour © Chad Ehlers/Alamy;
p.28 Orchard © Hemis/Alamy; **p.28** Assorted apples © Schnare & Stief/StockFood UK; **p.31** French market
© Cephas Picture Library/Alamy; **p.33** Saffron © Owen Franken/CORBIS; **p.36** Bowls of pasta © Christine
Webb/Alamy; **p.39** Italian delicatessen - Stef Lumley; **p.42** Raspberries on bush © Balfour Studios/Alamy;
p.42 Raspberry preserve © David Marsden/Photolibrary.com; **p.44** Potato field © Brian Hagiwara/Brand X
Pictures/Getty Images; **p.46** Cheese shop © Dave Bartruff/CORBIS; **p.46** Cabbages and cauliflowers © Sarah
M. Golonka/Botanica/Getty Images; **p.49** German breads and cakes © presse-bild-poss/Alamy; **p.51** Coffee
in glass © Ingolf Pompe 12/Alamy; **p.56** Red peppers and paprika powder © Gabula Art-Foto/StockFood
UK; **p.58** Norwegian lake and mountains © WoodyStock/Alamy; **p.58** Lingonberries © age fotostock/
SuperStock; **p.61** Anchovies © Mode Images Limited/Alamy; **p.63** Danish harbor © Michael
Juno/Alamy; **p.64** Wheat field © RIA Novosti/Alamy; **p.65** Caviar © Mark L. Stephenson/CORBIS;
p.66 Egyptian bakers © Dave Bartruff/CORBIS; **p.68** Aubergines © Arco Images GmbH/Alamy;
p.71 Doner kebab © FAN travelstock/Alamy; **p.72** Date palms © Murat Taner/Photographer's
Choice/Getty Images; **p.72** Bowls of spices © Dave Bartruff/CORBIS; **p.78** Meal on banana leaf
© Hornbil Images/Alamy; Indian fruit and vegetable market © Tim Gainey/Alamy; **p.82** Floating
market in Thailand © Free Agents Limited/CORBIS; **p.84** Cloves drying in sun © Gerald S. Cubitt/Bruce
Coleman Collection; **p.85** Bags at spice market © Adam Woolfitt/CORBIS; **p.86** Paddy field © Keren Su/
China Span/Getty Images; **p.89** Women using chopsticks © Peter Adams/Photographer's Choice/Getty Images;
p.90 Japanese pickles © directphoto.bz/Alamy; **p.92** Passion fruit © David Cook/blueshiftstudios/Alamy

Index